"I thought my uncle wasn't much of a gossip—turns out I was wrong."

"Jax cared for you very much. Part of his reason for selling was so you could have your freedom again."

Dylan tugged off his gloves. "Well, doesn't that just beat all? This ranch was my freedom. My home. By taking it away from me, he was taking away every last breath I had."

"He thought if you had a fresh start on your own ranch without the debt and problems of this place hanging over your head that you'd be able to move on.'

Dylan recoiled at her words. "Oh, you're good."

"I don't understand."

"Your job is to convince me to sell and you're using the information my uncle told you against me. I already know my uncle's final wish was to sell this place. Doesn't mean I'm going to honor it."

"Forget I said anything."

Emma stormed out of the stables leaving him alone wi

A SNOWBOUND COWBOY CHRISTMAS

BY
AMANDA RENEE

MILLS & BOON

First Published in Great Britain 2017
By Mills & Boon, an imprint of HarperCollins*Publishers*
1 London Bridge Street, London, SE1 9GF

© 2017 Amanda Renee

ISBN: 978-0-263-92350-6

23-1117

Our policy is to use papers that are natural, renewable and recyclable products and made from wood grown in sustainable forests. The logging and manufacturing processes conform to the legal environmental regulations of the country of origin.

Printed and bound in Spain
by CPI, Barcelona

Amanda Renee was raised in the northeast and now wriggles her toes in the warm coastal Carolina sands. Her career began when she was discovered through Mills & Boon So You Think You Can Write contest. When not creating stories about love and laughter, she enjoys the company of her schnoodle, Duffy, camping, playing guitar and piano, photography and anything involving horses. You can visit her at www.amandarenee.com.

To my editor, Johanna Raisanen:

Thank you for your invaluable
guidance on this book!

Chapter One

"I'm not selling you my ranch."

Emma Sheridan's skin prickled beneath her down parka at the sound of the voice behind her. She'd recognize it anywhere. *Dylan Slade*. They'd only met face-to-face once during the summer and had three or four brief phone conversations since, but his masculine resonance was impossible to forget. He was every man's cowboy and every woman's fantasy. Okay, maybe not every woman's, but he had snuck into her dreams a time or ten. Then again, it could just be her pregnancy hormones talking.

Emma handed her credit card to the front desk clerk at the Silver Bells Guest Ranch, and then turned to face Dylan. "Mr. Slade." Her breath caught at the realization he stood less than an arm's length away. "Please accept my sincerest sympathies. I only knew your Uncle Jax for a year, but he was a wonderful man with a generous heart."

"That he was." Dylan tugged off his work gloves and unzipped his whiskey-colored rancher jacket. "I appreciate your condolences, but it doesn't explain why you're here. We received your company's floral arrangement."

Emma cringed. She hated the customary funeral-home flowers her firm had sent. They were cold and impersonal. She'd mailed Dylan a hand-written card as well, but he didn't bother to mention it. Then again, why would he? Her visit wasn't to relay condolences in person. It was business. Business she needed to settle before her baby was born. She glanced up at him. His dark, well-worn cowboy hat shielded his eyes more than she'd have preferred. It made reading him difficult, which she assumed was intentional.

"I thought if we could talk—"

"You'd what? Change my mind? I'm not selling the ranch." He shrugged out of his coat as he strode past her, revealing faded snug Wranglers that fit him better than any pair of jeans had a right to. Inwardly, she groaned, relieved when he walked behind the lodge's rustic cedar-log front desk.

"You're all set, Ms. Sheridan." The check-in clerk slid her room key across the marred wood surface. An actual key. Her plans for the ranch included multiple guest-service agents and the latest digital room-entry technology. A guest's Bluetooth-enabled smartphone would become their room key via a downloadable app. "I'll have someone bring up your bags. Please help yourself to the complimentary snack bar in the dining room."

"Why are you staying here?" Dylan tilted back his hat, revealing an errant lock of chestnut-brown hair.

There was no mistaking his scowl now. "My decision isn't up for debate."

"You never heard my final proposal. At least hear me out." Emma shifted uncomfortably in her too-tight rubber duck boots. The shoes were far from fashionable, but they were snow-friendly and easy to slip on. At least, they had been before she boarded her redeye flight from Chicago to Saddle Ridge in northwestern Montana. Now she'd need a crowbar to pry them off. "Besides, Jax told me he hadn't booked any reservations after December in anticipation of closing this deal on January 2. It doesn't look like people are waiting in line for you to reopen, so what's the harm in discussing it?" A sharp internal kick to her ribs caused Emma to inhale. Her daughter had been super active today and the nerve-racking drive in the snow from the airport hadn't helped matters any. She had read that her unborn baby could sense her emotions and today definitely confirmed it. The doctor had told her it was safe to make the trip, but he had also warned it would be her last until after the baby was born. "I have to sit down."

As much as she wanted—correction, *needed*—to discuss the agreement Jax had made to sell the guest ranch, her feet had reached their limit. She tottered toward the lodge's great room. At thirty-two weeks pregnant, she envied the women who radiated in the pre-baby hormonal glow and managed to survive the entire nine months in a blissfully beautiful state of impending motherhood. She'd trade an ounce of their exuberance for her swollen feet and ankles, not to mention the other parts of her body that had seen better days.

"Are you all right?" Dylan's closeness startled her again. "Would you like a bottle of water?" He guided her by the arm to the most comfortable-looking chair she'd ever seen. "You look terrible."

Emma laughed, dropping her handbag at her feet. "You really shouldn't say that to a woman." She unfastened her jacket, not bothering to remove it as she sank into the burnished leather chair near the massive granite fireplace. *Oh, this is heaven.* She'd definitely need help to get up, but she'd worry about that later.

"You're pregnant." Dylan's deep blue eyes grew large as he stared at her protruding belly. "I had no idea."

Feeling exposed, Emma struggled to pull her parka closed over her fisherman-knit sweater. Of course, now she was sitting on half of the coat, which made the task impossible.

"Eight months." Emma rested her hands protectively on her stomach. "It's a girl, but I haven't chosen a name yet. I'm surprised your uncle didn't tell you." Jax had instinctively known, even though she hadn't begun to show when they'd spoken. He'd said her panicked smile gave it away. Well, that on top of the morning sickness and the constant heartburn she'd had during her visit.

Dylan shook his head. "My uncle may have been somewhat eccentric and unfiltered at times, but he wasn't a gossiping man. Not that your pregnancy is gossip."

That wasn't altogether true. The fact that her boy-friend of six months had ditched her the second he found out she was pregnant had made for great water-cooler gossip around the office. Especially since her job as a commercial real estate analyst hinged on her ability to fly anywhere in the world at a moment's notice. That ended with this trip.

She traveled as many as twenty days a month and while her job paid well, it didn't afford her the luxury of a nanny to accompany her and care for her baby while she was scouting resort locations or meeting with clients and investors. Once her daughter was born, she would be unable to meet the travel require-ments her job demanded. She had two options: accept a lesser position with less pay or get the acquisitions director promotion she'd been vying for and work solely from their Chicago corporate offices. Acquir-ing the Silver Bells Ranch almost guaranteed that promotion. She refused to give up now.

"Water would be great. Thank you." His exit gave her a chance to compose herself a little better and get out of her suffocating coat. The full-length parka was overkill for mid-December, but she wasn't taking any chances. Plus, wearing it beat trying to stuff it into another piece of luggage. By the time she freed her-self from its confines, Dylan had returned and she was perspiring profusely.

"Are you sure you're okay?" He handed her the bottle.

Emma twisted the cap off and took a long swallow. "I'm fine, thank you. It's just the warmth of the fireplace and this monstrosity of a coat."

Standing in front of her silhouetted by the midmorning sun filtering in through the floor-to-ceiling windows, Dylan epitomized tall, dark and sexy.

"Good. Then go home. I'm not selling."

And obstinate to the core. Emma had already decided she liked Dylan much better when he didn't speak. Unfortunately, getting him to sell his ranch was why she was there. She refused to leave until he did.

DYLAN HADN'T EVEN grieved yet for the man he had loved as a father. Jax had been in perfect health, which made his sudden heart attack even more shocking. He had wanted to hold on to the ranch and bring in a new business partner, but no one wanted to invest in an aging ranch. Not even his own brothers. A part of him wondered if the bickering he and Jax had done over the sale had contributed to his uncle's death. Now Silver Bells was his and he had to prove to himself that he'd been right to keep it all along.

Without steady revenue, he had to rely on what was left of his savings to float the business. Jax had stopped taking reservations months ago and Emma was right…no one was beating down their door to get in. They hadn't been for more than a year—and the instant the ranch had taken a downturn, she had swooped in and offered to buy it.

Emma bordered between a vixen and a cherub. Her intelligence coupled with her persistence had hooked Jax from their first meeting. At five and a half feet, she wasn't overly tall or bombshell curvaceous. Instead, the brunette had a wicked grin that usually ended in a friendly wink. She exuded charm along with a street-savvy wit that left those around her intoxicated by her performance. And it was a performance designed to lull potential sellers into a euphoric sense of *everything would be wonderful* once they closed the deal. She was a brilliant saleswoman and Dylan understood why she was so successful, but he could also see right through her.

Today, her perfectly manicured facade had a crack in it. But that crack made her appear more natural and she wore it well, despite her obvious discomfort. She winced for the second time since her arrival. The ranch should be the least of her concerns, and she had to be the least of his. He didn't have the patience to deal with a pushy pregnant woman, let alone one who should be relaxing at home choosing baby names.

"Isn't your husband worried about you?"

"Thanks for the concern, but I'm not married, attached or otherwise. It's just me and the butter bean."

"Butter bean? That's what you call your kid?"

Emma rubbed her belly and smiled up at him. Any man worth his salt could get lost in her bourbon-colored eyes if he wasn't careful. Good thing he'd sworn off women with kids years ago.

"I have craved butter beans since the beginning of my pregnancy. That's how I found out I was expecting. A friend jokingly asked if I was pregnant. Biggest surprise of my life."

"And the father?" Dylan held up his hands. "No, I'm sorry. That's none of my business."

"It's no secret. He left two seconds after I told him." She tilted her chin up defiantly. "I had his parental rights terminated shortly thereafter. He didn't fight it and my baby is better off this way. I'd never force my daughter on a man who wants nothing to do with her."

"I give you a lot of credit." It pained him whenever he heard a man had relinquished his paternal rights to a child. Dylan had wanted kids and a family more than anything. He'd lived that dream, and then he lost it after he'd partnered with Jax on Silver Bells. His ex-wife had warned him she wouldn't like living on a ranch. Stubbornly, he thought he'd change her mind. Lauren had tried her best, but living in an outdated log cabin away from her family and friends proved to be too much. She packed up his two stepkids and moved back to Bozeman. No way would he raise another man's child again. It was too heartbreaking when it didn't work out.

Lauren and the kids leaving, coupled with his father's death a few months later, damn near broke him. From then on, he devoted every waking hour to the ranch. He and Jax had updated what they could afford to, and the Silver Bells did great until more guest ranches cropped up nearby. They couldn't compete with the new.

"It's all good," she said.

Her robotic response told him otherwise, but he couldn't allow that to matter. Dylan squatted next to her chair and rested a hand on her arm. He immediately regretted the close contact, even though her bulky sweater separated her skin from his palm. It was bad enough her almond-scented shampoo left him wanting to bury his face in the long silky strands. He found this vulnerable side of Emma endearing when he knew to avoid her. She was off-limits in far too many ways.

"I admire your strength and fortitude to see this deal come to fruition but, Emma, it won't happen. I went along with my uncle because he owned the majority stake in the business. I didn't have a choice then. There are a few options I'm mulling over, but selling to you isn't on the list." Dylan stood and walked to the windows overlooking the ranch. "This is a guest ranch where people come to be cowboys and cowgirls for a week or two. It will never be the luxurious five-star spa resort you want to turn it into."

"Um, excuse me. Some help over here," Emma called behind him.

He turned to find her struggling to stand and couldn't help but laugh a little. She was cute when she was vulnerable. He closed the distance between them and offered both his hands. Their eyes met as he pulled her to her feet and inadvertently against his body.

"Sorry," he mumbled before stepping back.

A tinge of pink flooded her cheeks as she smoothed her sweater. "Would you rather turn your employees out on the street?"

The woman didn't miss a beat. "You and my uncle

already have." Dylan headed toward the front desk, sensing her close behind him. "Some already left to secure work somewhere else. When my uncle announced that the ranch would close its doors on January 1, many of our employees began searching for work elsewhere. Some found positions, while others planned on staying until the end. I've already told them Silver Bells isn't closing, and I'll do whatever I can to keep them employed here. We have families living on the ranch. Did my uncle tell you that? And some of my employees worked on my father's ranch before his death. I've known many of these people my entire life."

Emma shook her head. "I didn't know."

"I can't tell you how many marriages have taken place amongst the Silver Bells employees. We have another in a few days, don't we, Sandy?" Dylan wrapped his arm around a dining-room server who had been passing by. "Sandy's the one getting married. Her fiancé, Luke, is a ranch hand here." Dylan continued into the kitchen. "Hopefully this won't be the last wedding. Many babies have been born here, too. Some of the kids raised on Silver Bells are raising families of their own on the ranch and you want to take that away. I can't understand why my uncle agreed to any of it. I just thank God he hadn't finalized anything."

"We were scheduled to in fifteen days." Emma lifted her chin. "And your employees can reapply once the renovations are completed."

Sandy scoffed at her statement. "Your company

refused to guarantee us employment. You can't expect us to go without any income or health insurance for six months."

"Many of the people working here live paycheck-to-paycheck," Dylan said over his shoulder as he walked to the pantry. His father had taught him to treat his employees like family and the thought of them suffering aggravated him further. He needed distance from Emma before he said something he'd regret.

"I'm sure we can work something out." She followed him, unrelenting. "Maybe a severance package."

"To cover six months? I highly doubt that." He hoisted a case of water onto his shoulder and faced her. "Listen. I'm not going to change my mind. So please, catch the first flight out of here because you're wasting your time pursuing this further. If you'll excuse me, I have a lot to do since we're shorthanded."

"Uh, Dylan? She's not going anywhere," Sandy said from the kitchen doorway. "Harlan just called. They closed all the roads because of this storm and we're expecting another foot of snow by tomorrow morning."

"You've got to be kidding me." But he knew she wasn't. His brother was a deputy sheriff and he would have heard the news directly from the Department of Transportation. "We're snowed in?"

"And here I thought Montana laughed in the face of snow." Emma stared at him with a confident smile and her arms folded above her baby bump. "The roads wouldn't be an issue if we owned the property."

Dylan set the water on the stainless-steel counter. "I have news for you. Saddle Ridge is a small town and we don't have the equipment to plow roads as fast as Chicago or even Kalispell and Whitefish."

"That's why we planned on donating two new snowplows to the town, ensuring the roads leading to the resort would be kept clear."

"It's a ranch. Not a resort." A fact she needed to get through her head. "And who is going to pay for the manpower to run those plows?"

"It's only two plows, Dylan." She toddled over to the counter and leaned against it, looking more tired than before. "We're talking about two drivers, four if they are running two shifts. I doubt it will bankrupt the town. They're getting new equipment and they are thrilled with the idea."

"Thrilled? You've already spoken with them?" Of course she had. He didn't think there was anything business-related she had overlooked, except the human side of the equation.

"Months ago. Your uncle even went with me to my Department of Transportation meeting. I assumed you knew."

"No. No, I didn't." He wondered what else he didn't know about the sale. "It doesn't matter now. The deal is off."

"Well, since it doesn't appear I'm leaving anytime soon, why don't we talk about that?"

"I hope you enjoy your stay, Ms. Sheridan, but I assure you, we will never have that conversation." The last thing Dylan needed was to be snowbound with the woman determined to take his ranch. Hell would freeze over before he'd let that happen.

Chapter Two

Emma couldn't believe her luck. If mother nature hadn't intervened, she was certain Dylan would have tossed her off the ranch. The storm hadn't been a surprise. She had been carefully watching the weather since last night, hoping the airline wouldn't cancel her flight. As much as she needed a reason to stay on the ranch, the snowed-in part made her nervous. She hadn't had any complications with her pregnancy, but she still wanted access to a hospital in case something did happen. Back home in Chicago, her apartment was six blocks from the hospital. The steady stream of sirens and medevac helicopters had become second nature to her. Most of the time she didn't hear them.

She glanced around the small room. It had seen better decades, but it was clean and tidy. Leaving her bags by the door, she took her laptop case and purse to the small round table by the window. Despite the hardness of the chair, she was happy to sit down again. After prying off her shoes, she propped up her feet on the chair across from her and set up her computer. She wanted to get as much work done as possible in case the lodge lost power. And judging by the looks of the place, the possibility was very real.

She typed a quick text message to her boss.

Made it to Silver Bells. Bad storm. Having hard time getting cell service. Hope this message gets through. Will try calling again later.

Providing no one from her office called the lodge directly, which she doubted they would, her white lie would go unnoticed. She pressed send, shut off her phone and tossed it on the table. Between yesterday's conference calls with their investors on the project and this morning's call from her boss when she landed, she'd had all the pressure she could stand. She needed time to work on her strategy. The ranch was still grieving Jax's death and there was a fine line between being aggressive and being obnoxious. Judging by Sandy's reaction to her in the dining room, her presence wasn't a welcome one. And she totally understood where they were coming from. Dylan wanted to protect his livelihood and she wanted to protect hers.

Her daughter thumped against her lower left rib. "Easy, butter bean. You're going to leave your mommy black and blue before you're born." Emma rubbed her belly. "We'll be home soon. Once I close this deal and get my promotion, your future will be secure and I can spend the rest of my pregnancy shopping for your arrival. I can't wait to meet you."

Despite the discomfort, her pregnancy had already

gone faster than she had imagined. A little too fast, considering all she had to do. There were only eight weeks left and she hadn't even started working on the nursery. She had no one to rely on except herself. Until this deal closed, she couldn't afford to ease up. Raising a baby alone was hard enough. It was even harder in a big city, and she refused to let her daughter down.

She had managed to pick up a few outfits during her business trips. Traveling hadn't given her much of a chance to shop, but she loved the idea of buying her daughter dresses from all over the world. It was something she wouldn't be able to do once she got her promotion. She had mixed emotions about not traveling anymore. As much as she loved it, she found it exhausting.

Making plans with friends had become a rare luxury over the years. She'd lost touch with many of them and looked forward to reconnecting with them once she had a more normal schedule. Many had families of their own and play dates with her daughter beat traipsing across the globe any day. But unless she got to work now, none of that would happen. She focused her attention on her laptop screen and began reviewing her notes.

An hour later, Emma stood and stretched. Her skin felt grimy from the flight and she wanted to slip into something less bulky and hot. She peeked into the bathroom. It wasn't lavish by any means, but it was spotless. And that suited her just fine.

Emma had just finished showering and dressing when she heard a knock on her room door. She opened it, startled to see Dylan holding a miniature decorated Christmas tree.

"This is a surprise." Emma had heard of waving the white flag, but never waving a Christmas tree. Nonetheless, she appreciated the effort. "How sweet!"

"All of our guests get a tree during the holidays. Normally they are in the room before they arrive, but since we hadn't booked this room before your unexpected visit, we hadn't bothered. Everyone deserves a little Christmas cheer."

Even her. He hadn't said the words, but they were certainly implied. So much for assuming he had done something just for her. Not that it mattered.

"Thank you." Emma took the tree from him and sat it on the worn oak dresser. "I'm hoping to be home by Christmas. You don't really think we'll still be snowed in then, do you? That's a week away." Not that she had any big plans. Her mother always said it was a kids' holiday and once she became an adult, they didn't do much to celebrate it. However, she still didn't want to spend her rare day off stuck in No-Man's-Land, Montana with the Grinch.

"I certainly hope not. But it has been unusually cold this year and this is our second snow storm of the season. Let's not even think about the possibility. I'm sure you'll be back home before you know it. Anyway, that thing lights up." Dylan crossed the room like he owned the place—which he did—and eased between her and the tree. The slight brush of his body against hers caused the hair on the back of her neck to stand on end. Of course, he probably wouldn't have touched her if her belly hadn't been in the way. She had never felt more unattractive in her life. He wiggled the dresser from the wall to access the outlet and bent over, allowing her the perfect view of his backside. At least that brought a smile to her face.

"There you go." He moved the dresser back into place and admired the tree as if he'd been the one to invent the electric light. "Now you're all set."

Dylan tilted back his hat. "I don't know if anyone had the chance to tell you our meal schedule around here. Breakfast runs from six to eight, lunch is at noon and dinner at six. Breakfast and lunch are buffets and we serve dinner family-style, where everyone eats together. Although I'm sure you already know what our lodge has to offer. While it's not sushi and escargot, I assure you it's stick-to-your-ribs good food."

"Great." Emma had never been fond of the whole meat-and-potatoes thing. After wining and dining corporate clients in some of the finest restaurants in the world, her taste buds had been spoiled. She tried to muster some enthusiasm. "I look forward to it." She was already hungry and at this point, she couldn't afford to be picky.

"I notified the staff that you may have some extra needs." Dylan jammed his hands into his pockets and glanced around the room. Was it possible that Mr. Surly was nervous being alone with a pregnant woman? Emma privately laughed at the thought. "We're not a fancy resort with a twenty-four-hour kitchen, but our head chef said he'd make you some pre-prepared snacks that you will be able to heat up very quickly in the microwave down there. Just tell him your preferences. I know it's not the greatest, but we haven't had too many pregnant guests stay here. We're a little unprepared. I'm sure pre-baby vacations were part of your luxury resort spa, weren't they?"

"They were." Emma would give anything for a little pampering. "I appreciate the extra effort you're making on my behalf, but it's not necessary. I don't want to put anybody out."

"You're not putting us out." There was no disguising Dylan's double meaning. "The staff is good about keeping the walkways clear at all times, but I've asked them to be vigilant with the ice melt. So, if you do go outside, you won't slip and fall. They will continually recheck it during the day, especially in the mornings."

"Thank you." Emma thought about her company's plans for the ranch. It included heated walkways, ensuring guests could safely walk from one area of the resort to the other.

He tugged his hat down low, shielding his eyes. "I'm just being hospitable. After all, this is a guest ranch and you're a guest." He turned his back to her and strode to the open door. "Let my staff know if you need anything."

Before she could respond further, he was gone. Despite his gruffness, she found his gesture endearing. Not that he'd ever admit to it being more than his job. Because they both knew he could have sent anyone up with a tree or forgotten about it altogether. Either way, she was there to convince him to sell the ranch, not make friends.

DYLAN KICKED HIMSELF for going to her room. The only reason he had was because she'd looked exhausted earlier and he wanted to make sure she was all right. That was his job as the ranch owner. He could've insisted an employee drop off the tree and report back to him. The thought had crossed his mind, but he vetoed it because Emma had managed to make quite a few enemies on the ranch. It was hard enough adjusting to life without Jax. Everyone had begun to breathe again when he told them he wasn't selling Silver Bells. Now her presence brought up myriad speculations. He'd spent the better part of an hour reassuring everyone he hadn't changed his mind. He didn't have extra time for that, but he'd had to make the time. Instead, he needed to focus on finding another investor in the ranch if he wanted to keep rooves over his employees' heads. It irked him that Emma was there. Now he felt responsible for her while they were snowed in and she was one more aggravation he didn't need.

It was almost noon when Dylan hopped on one of the ranch's snowmobiles and headed toward the stables. Nothing cured a man's worries like honest hard work. He shut the engine off in front of the first building. With almost a hundred horses in residence, they had four separate stables in a row with the last building reserved mostly for maintenance. The weathered barn siding had faded to a light gray over the years. They needed updating along with the rest of the ranch. Dylan had tried to allocate money equally between the horses and the lodge, but there just wasn't enough to go around.

When you didn't have a whole lot of money, it meant you always had work to do. Considering they were short-staffed after many of their employees had decided to leave when Jax announced the ranch's imminent closing, Dylan had been pulling double duty. But he needed the distraction of extra work now more than anything.

One of the stables still hadn't been mucked thanks to Wes once again skipping out on work. In hindsight, he should've fired his brother a long time ago, but Dylan and Jax had been the only ranch around willing to put up with his extensive bull-riding schedule. He'd thought after the World Finals that Wes would have returned to work full-time again. He'd been mistaken. At least his brother had the courtesy to send him a text message and say he wasn't coming in. He didn't even know where the man was sleeping anymore. He had a cabin on the ranch, but he rarely stayed in it.

He couldn't blame Wes for not wanting to stick around. Their family had fractured the moment their father had died. Correction, had been killed. His brother, Ryder, had confessed to running over their father after a drunken argument. Four and a half years later and it still didn't make sense to him. Ryder and their father had always had a great relationship. He had never seen them argue let alone get into a drunken brawl. It didn't matter now. Dylan had been forced to accept it. He just wished it hadn't destroyed the rest of his family. He still couldn't bring himself to visit his brother in prison.

His mother had sold the family ranch and moved to California shortly after the funeral. She'd remarried a year ago and had no plans of returning. His other brother, Garrett, had moved to Wyoming with his wife years earlier and Wes devoted ninety-nine percent of his time to bull riding. That left only Dylan and Harlan in Saddle Ridge. Jax had become a second father to them both. And now he was gone, too.

Dylan reached into his back pocket for his work gloves and realized he'd left them in his truck. He grabbed a spare pair from the tack room and set off in search of the wheelbarrow. He'd already fed the horses that morning. Normally the stalls were empty this time of day, but he'd kept the horses inside when he'd seen the weather report. Mucking stalls when you had to continually move horses around was a pain in the ass. Between that, repairing some tack, ordering supplies and a second attempt at fixing one of their ranch trucks, it would be well past sunset before he finished for the day. Good. That's what he wanted. No—it's what he needed.

Over the past six months, Dylan felt like what was left of his family had splintered even further. After Harlan and his ex-wife had split up, whenever he was on late-night patrol as deputy sheriff, Dylan used to babysit his daughter, Ivy. Now that Harlan had married Belle, she watched Ivy when he wasn't home. There were still rare instances when they both had work or were in desperate need of a date night, but it wasn't like it used to be. He missed spending time with his niece. Combined with many of his friends leaving the ranch and Jax's death, he had never felt more alone.

Dylan snatched a shovel from the wall bracket and swung open a stall door. He jammed it into the soiled hay and tossed it into the wheelbarrow. By the time he reached the last stall in the first stable, he no longer felt the cold. Hay and manure replaced the sweet scent of Emma's hair. A blister had begun to form between his thumb and index finger and he welcomed the ache. If only it would replace the one that had settled deep within his heart.

Five years ago, he had been a man-with-a-plan. He had bought into Silver Bells with the best of intentions. Jax had owned the ranch for three decades and it made a solid income. But he'd had plans to make it better. Together, they were going to create the biggest and best family guest ranch in the state of Montana. His ex, Lauren, had told him repeatedly that she didn't want to live on a ranch. She wanted to stay in her modern home with sheetrock walls, not rough-hewn cedar logs. She wanted neighbors and a two-car garage, not hundreds of acres for a backyard. And the horses… She'd warned him she wasn't an animal person, yet he had pushed and pushed until finally she'd pushed back and left.

In hindsight, they couldn't have been more opposites of each other. It's what had attracted him to her in the first place. She wasn't a big city girl like

Emma, but she was definitely suburbia. Dylan had made a name for himself training horses and he had set aside every penny he'd made, earning interest. When he'd met Lauren, she'd been divorced for a solid two years already. She had two kids—a boy and a girl, ages three and five. Sweet as the day was long. He loved those kids as if they were his own. And they loved him enough to call him dad. It made her leaving that much harder.

Maybe it wouldn't have been so bad if their marriage had started on a ranch. If he had let her know from the beginning that this was the life he wanted. Instead, he had moved into her traditional four-bedroom home in Bozeman. The city was touristy, rugged and quaint all in the same breath. He had found work but felt suffocated living in their cookie-cutter housing development. The only time he had felt at home during their marriage was when he was working on someone else's ranch. So, when Jax had presented him with the opportunity to partner in Silver Bells, he jumped on it.

Lauren had followed him faithfully, despite her protests. The day they sold her house, she bawled like he'd never seen before. That had been his first sign they may not last. Dylan hadn't touched any of the money from that sale. His conscience wouldn't allow him to. That decision had given Lauren the financial freedom to leave.

The kids had been seven and nine when they moved to the ranch. They had been excited at first, but had quickly grown bored of ranch life when they realized they couldn't run down the street to play with their friends. Lauren missed her book club and Board of Education administration position. She'd accepted an office job in town, but she couldn't relate to the other women and their laid-back country lifestyle. The connection just wasn't there.

She had stuck it out for a year. An actual year to the day. And then that was it. He hadn't tried to stop her when she left. There had been no point. She was better off without him. Happier, at least. And the last he'd heard, she had married a Bozeman businessman and had returned to living in a cookie-cutter housing development with manicured lawns and white vinyl fences.

He didn't blame her. He blamed himself. He'd made her believe he was somebody other than he was. It didn't make losing her and the kids any easier. Since he hadn't legally adopted the children, he had no claim to them. He'd been their father for four years and he missed it as much today as he had when she'd left.

"I don't think I've ever seen a real live cowboy at work."

Emma's voice startled him and he almost impaled himself on the shovel.

"Somebody has to do it around here since you ran off my men." Dylan blew out a hard breath. "I didn't mean that."

"Yeah, you kind of did. But I get it. No harm, no f— What is that smell?"

"Manure."

"Does it always stink so bad?"

Dylan started laughing so hard he had to brace himself against the stall door. "It's pretty rank, but I think it might smell stronger because you're pregnant. But don't throw up in this stall, I just finished cleaning it."

"I'm way past the morning-sickness stage. Thank God," she mumbled while trying to hold her breath.

A gentleman would have offered to walk away from the manure-filled wheelbarrow so she could breathe again, but he wasn't feeling very gentlemanly. Maybe she would hate the smell enough and wait for him in the stable office until he could find someone to drive her back to the lodge.

"What can I do for you, Emma?" He purposely walked close to her as he passed so she could get a good whiff of him, knowing he wasn't playing very fair. "How did you get out here, anyway?"

"Your brother gave me a ride."

"Wes is here?" Dylan tugged off his gloves and yanked his phone out of his pocket. "That son of a— He should be the one doing this, not me. Did he come in with you?"

Emma shook her head. "No. He's plowing the ranch roads. I don't think he plans on working in the stables right now."

At least his brother had decided to work after all. "I love how I own the ranch and I'm the one doing the grunt work. So, I guess now you're stuck out here with me. I don't have time to drive you back and I certainly don't have time to entertain you."

"I'm not asking you to entertain me."

"Why are you out here, Emma?"

"Kindly lose the attitude. I realize I'm not your favorite person. All I'm asking for is a couple hours of your time to hear my proposal."

"You have a lot of nerve, sweetheart." He couldn't believe her attitude. "I know all about your plans for the ranch."

"No, Dylan, you don't. You think you do, but you don't. How do I know? Because I never pitched them to you, and Jax told me you didn't want to listen to him. You might feel differently if we talked about it."

"As you can already see, I don't have a couple hours to spare." Dylan tossed his shovel on top of the wheelbarrow and began pushing it down the stable corridor. "Honestly, I'm finding your insistence insulting."

"I—I never meant to offend you." Emma backed away from him and straight into one of the open stall doors.

"Be careful." He sighed. "Listen, I know you're just doing your job. I apologize for my attitude. You being here is bringing up some memories I would rather have kept in the past. And before you ask, no, I don't want to talk about them."

"Is this about your ex-wife?"

Dylan abruptly released the handles of the wheelbarrow, almost causing it to tip over. "How the hell do you know about that?"

"Jax told me your wife and kids left because you

moved them out here and that's a big reason why you didn't want to sell the ranch."

"You're half-right. My wife and *her* kids. And there's more to my not wanting to sell than that. Here I thought my uncle wasn't much of a gossip. Turns out I was wrong."

"Jax cared for you very much. Part of his reason for selling was so you could have your freedom again."

Dylan tugged off his gloves. "Well, doesn't that just beat all? This ranch was my freedom. My home. By taking it away from me, he was taking away the last breath I had. Did he really say that to you?"

Emma nodded slowly, closing the distance between them. "He thought if you had a fresh start on your own ranch without the debt and problems of this place hanging over your head that you'd be able to move on."

Dylan recoiled at her words. "Oh, you're good."

"I don't understand."

"Your job is to convince me to sell and you're using the information my uncle told you against me." He had known she was a shrewd businesswoman; he hadn't known she'd take it this far. "I already know my uncle's final wish was to sell this place. Doesn't mean I'm going to honor it, and your charms will not convince me otherwise."

"You want to be mad at me for being here? Go right ahead. You want to be mad that Jax died? Do it. Let it out. Scream, shout, kick something. It's okay to be mad at the past. But please don't insult me in the process."

Emma stormed out of the stables, leaving him alone with nothing but a pile of manure.

"THE NERVE OF that man," Emma grumbled to herself as she traipsed down the freshly-plowed road toward the lodge. She could just about make out the roof of the building from where she stood. At least there was a lull in the storm and it had stopped snowing. While the exercise felt good, her feet were beginning to ache and her fingers were cold. She reached inside her pocket for her phone. Maybe if she called the lodge, somebody could come get her.

She pulled off a glove with her teeth and began to scroll through her contacts when she heard an engine coming up behind her. She stepped off the road and into a pile of cold, wet snow that instantly seeped down into her duck boot moccasins. After she'd let out a few choice curse words, the snowmobile stopped in front of her and cut the engine.

Dylan.

"I don't want to talk to you." Emma stomped onto the path in a vain attempt to shake the snow from her shoes. She only succeeded in shaking it farther down toward her toes.

"I don't want to talk to you either, but I'm not going to allow you to freeze out here. You were crazy to think you could walk back to the lodge in this weather."

Emma wanted to ignore him, but she was too cold and no amount of pride was worth freezing over. "I was just calling the lodge to have someone come and get me."

"I'm your somebody. Hop on."

"Hop on where?" While the snowmobile was a decent size, there was no way her and her belly would fit behind him. At least not without her holding on to him for dear life.

Dylan scooted forward to make more room. "Get on. I'll go slow, I promise."

Emma raked her hands down her face. She had never been snowmobiling in her life and she didn't think her doctor back home in Chicago would approve of this little outdoor activity. She climbed on behind him and gripped his hips.

"Wrap your arms around me," Dylan said over his shoulder.

"I can't. My stomach is in the way," Emma muttered.

She didn't hear or see Dylan laughing, but she felt his body reverberating against hers. She smacked his arm. "It's not funny. You try being pregnant."

"I'm sorry." He continued to laugh. "Can you hold on to my shoulders?"

Emma slid her hands up his back, relishing the solid muscle beneath her palms. "I can handle that."

"Apparently." Dylan arched against her as she squeezed his shoulders.

"You stink." His odor was probably her only saving grace. If he had smelled musky and manly, she might not have been able to control herself. And she wouldn't have been able to blame it on her pregnancy hormones.

By the time they reached the lodge, she needed another change of clothes. She didn't want to sit down to dinner smelling like… Dylan. She wanted to make a graceful escape from the back of the snowmobile—unfortunately getting on was easier than getting off. The story of her pregnancy.

After Dylan's assistance, she managed to break free of him. "Thank you for the ride." She headed into the lodge. She may have been grateful for the ride, but she was still mad at him.

"Emma, wait."

She didn't bother to stop. She'd had enough of Dylan Slade for one day.

Chapter Three

Emma hadn't realized she'd slept through dinner
until she heard a soft knock at the door. If her stomach hadn't been grumbling, she would've ignored it.
She couldn't deal with another minute of Dylan this
evening. She checked the peephole, surprised to see
Sandy standing in the hallway holding a tray.

She unlocked the door and eased it open. "I'm
sorry, I fell asleep."

"That's okay. I figured that's what happened so I
brought you dinner. May I come in?" Emma stepped
aside as the petite brunette entered the room and set
the tray on the small table near the window. "I wanted
to apologize for the way I spoke to you earlier. I'm a
little frazzled with my Christmas Day wedding coming up. It's no excuse, though."

"Believe me, I realize I'm the enemy. We're on
opposite sides. It's cool. I do hope you have the wedding of your dreams."

"Thanks." Sandy tucked a piece of hair behind her
ear that had worked its way loose from her French
braid. "There's a little bit of everything on here. If you

want more, just ring downstairs. I see Dylan brought you up the Christmas tree. I know he's a little gruff on the outside, but he really is a big teddy bear once you get to know him."

"Somehow I don't think anyone's going to mistake Dylan for a squishable stuffed animal anytime soon."

"Then I guess you won't mind me telling you he was the one who fixed your tray." Sandy winked as she walked into the hallway. "I live here in the lodge. Extension 307. Call me if you need anything."

"Thanks, I will." Emma closed the door.

Dylan fixed her tray? She eyed it warily. "I wonder what he did to it."

She lifted the plate to remove the plastic wrap and found a folded note.

I'm sorry for earlier.
Dylan.

Well, that was unexpected. The smell of fried chicken, mashed potatoes and gravy got the best of her. And then she saw them…butter beans. *He remembered.* There was also a huge slab of chocolate cake, macaroni and cheese and a slice of meatloaf. Classic comfort food. She'd never desired it until this very moment. And she planned to eat every ounce of it or explode trying.

Halfway through her meal, her text-message tone sounded from the other side of the table. She'd forgotten to turn her phone back off after calling her best friend, Jennie, to help forget her argument with

Dylan. She wanted to ignore it, but she was already full anyway. She reached for her phone and tapped the screen to see a message from her boss.

Conference call tomorrow. 1 p.m. Chicago time. Want update.

Her boss had a penchant for caveman text messaging and emails. She didn't know if she was supposed to call him or he was supposed to call her. Either way, it wouldn't be a good conversation. At least it gave her the morning to prepare for it. She would have preferred to wait until after Dylan heard her proposal, if she could ever convince him to give her half a chance. Maybe her boss could offer some insight on how to change Dylan's mind, although that felt as if she were admitting she didn't have any ideas of her own.

Emma would have preferred staying in her room for the rest of the night, but she didn't think Silver Bells had tray pick up, especially since they didn't offer room service. While she was down there, she'd find out about laundry service or the use of a washing machine and dryer.

Carrying her tray down a flight of stairs proved to be more precarious than she'd anticipated. She couldn't wait for her center of gravity to be back where it belonged. By the time she reached the kitchen, she'd broken out into a cold sweat. Thankfully, she hadn't made a scene by dropping the tray along the way.

A group of around twenty people had gathered near the fireplace while someone played guitar and sang "Jingle Bell Rock." She loved that song. It had always put her in a festive holiday mood. She walked toward the small crowd, singing along until she caught a glimpse of who was playing. Dylan. Of course, it had to be Dylan.

A slow easy grin settled over his face as his eyes met hers. He continued to sing, and for a moment, everyone else disappeared. When the song ended, their applause jolted her back to reality. Good thing it was only a fantasy, because the last thing she wanted was to be alone with Dylan again. They'd kissed and made up and that was good enough for her. *Kissed?* No! She could not think about kissing Dylan Slade.

Absolutely not.

Not going to happen.

Not even in her dreams.

Okay, so she had kissed him in her dreams once before. But that was then and this was now.

He began playing Brooks & Dunn's "Hangin' 'Round the Mistletoe," which sounded dangerously sexy when Dylan sang it. He had a great voice. It didn't help that he still hadn't broken eye contact. She wanted to look away first, but she couldn't will herself to do so. That was until she noticed everyone else was staring at her. Great. Now she felt even more self-conscious. And then she realized why she was the center of attention. Hanging above her head was none other than a sprig of mistletoe. Double crap!

DYLAN ENDED THE song to a round of applause. He placed the house guitar back on the stand where anyone was welcome to play it. Emma had latched herself on to two other female guests, probably to avoid him. And who could blame her.

The three of them disappeared, leaving him to wonder if he would see Emma again tonight. Dylan attempted to mingle with the ranch's guests. They didn't have a full house, but they had managed to fill almost a dozen rooms. Instead of making small talk or thinking about Emma, he needed to focus on finding a new investor. The road closures meant the kids living on the ranch wouldn't have school. He'd bribe them to muck the stalls tomorrow if his brother didn't show up for work again. There was no point in saying anything to Wes, because he never stayed around long enough for it to matter. That didn't mean the responsibility of the horses was going away anytime soon.

He still couldn't get what Emma had told him about Jax out of his head. Had his uncle truly believed selling the ranch was in Dylan's best interest? It would have been different if Lauren had left a few months ago. Then maybe he could have salvaged his marriage. In the end, it probably would have only been a temporary bandage. Sometimes you couldn't fix what wasn't meant to be.

When Emma reappeared, he could have sworn his heart quickened. But that was impossible, unless it was out of aggravation. A part of him wanted to find out what else Jax had said to her about him, but the other part figured he was better off not knowing. Sandy and Luke interrupted his thoughts when they carried out two large trays of s'mores fixings and told the guests to grab their jackets and follow them outside.

A fire was already burning in the stone fire pit behind the lodge. A light snow continued to fall as flames danced between him and Emma while Sandy showed her how to make the melted chocolate, toasted marshmallow and graham cracker sandwich. For someone as worldly as he thought she was, he found it funny that she had never made s'mores before. Then again, she was a city girl.

At least Sandy had apologized for earlier. Which is what he had hoped she would do when he asked her to bring Emma a tray of food. It was one thing for him to be annoyed she was there, but she was a guest and his employees needed to respect that.

"Oh, my God! These are amazing!" Emma happily squealed. Sandy placed her reindeer antlers headband on Emma's head as Luke stuck another marshmallow on the end of her stick.

Dylan felt like a kid looking through the window of a birthday party he hadn't been invited to. He wanted to share in their laughter. Dylan shook the thought from his brain. In a few days, he would never see or speak to Emma again. Good. So why did that thought bother him? She had her life in the big city and he had his in rural Montana. And if there was one thing he knew for sure, the two didn't mix.

"Thank you for dinner." Emma managed to startle him once again.

"You really need to stop sneaking up on people."

"What people? And you were looking right at me."

Emma shook her head. "I won't take up any of your time. I just wanted to say thank you for your apology and I accept."

Dylan tried not to laugh at the bells jingling on her antlers as she spoke. "I'm taking some of the guests on a snowcat tour of the ranch in a little while. I have room for one more if you care to join us?"

"Is that the giant red boxy-looking vehicle with the tracks I saw near the stables earlier?"

"Yep. We give tours a couple times a day. We're just coming off a new moon, and if it was a clear night, you'd be able to see a million stars. And every once in a while, we're able to see the northern lights. Because of the snow and the low visibility, we're just driving around the ranch tonight."

"I'd love to go, but I don't think I can get my butt up into that thing."

"There are steps in the back. It's easy and perfectly safe. We don't go fast at all."

"Sure, sounds like fun. It will be another first for me."

"Like s'mores?" Dylan envisioned Emma having a running checklist of things she had to accomplish in life.

"Hey now, not everyone grew up around campfires." *Jingle, jingle.*

"Fair enough. We'll leave here at ten. The tour is about an hour."

"Great, I look forward to it." She gave him a slight wink as she smiled. That was the Emma smile he remembered the first day they met. It had transfixed him even then. He needed to get it out of his head and fast before he found himself agreeing to her ideas as Jax had.

Once Dylan began loading everyone into the snow-cat, he realized they had booked more people than he had thought. By the time Emma made it outside, the only place left for her to sit was up front next to him. He had wanted to be hospitable, not have her inches away from him in the cab of his favorite diesel toy.

"I thought you said there were steps." Emma said as he helped her climb onto the track and into the cab, already regretting her close proximity.

"That's when I thought fewer people were coming along tonight." Dylan made a mental note to double-check future reservations before offering to take her along anyplace else. He closed her door and hopped into the driver's side.

"Where's the steering wheel?" Emma asked once she settled in her seat.

"There isn't one." Dylan laughed. He had asked Jax the same question when he first learned how to drive the vehicle. His uncle had picked it up used at auction for a ridiculously low price. They couldn't have afforded it any other way. The tours were a nice package addition to offer their guests. Newer ranches might be sprouting up around them, but they didn't have snowcat tours. And they didn't have the acreage that Silver Bells had.

Dylan started the engine and gripped both control sticks. "Almost every part of a snowcat is controlled by hydraulics. When I turn left, the right track speeds up and pushes the vehicle to the left. Same thing if we're turning right."

"I don't see a brake pedal." Emma leaned toward him to get a better look, giving him an inadvertent chance to smell her hair. There it was again. Almonds.

"It doesn't have that, either. Snowcats are super heavy. By letting off the gas or pulling back on the control sticks, it slows to a stop. It does have a parking brake, though, if that makes you feel any better."

"I'm surprised how warm it is in here. I expected to freeze."

"These vehicles are designed for subzero temperatures. Even the windshield is heated to prevent icing. Providing there's diesel to power it, you'll stay nice and warm in this thing."

Emma continued to ask questions until they reached the far side of the ranch, overlooking the town of Saddle Ridge.

"This is normally where I let everyone out to walk around and take some night photography shots. Since the snow is so light, I'm going to check in the back to see if anyone wants to get out."

"I could stand to get out and walk around a little. I think I'm wearing every item of clothing I brought with me. I'm about ready to roast."

"Just let me make sure the snow is hard-packed enough. I don't want to chance you falling."

Dylan unloaded his passengers out of the back door of the snowcat before returning to Emma. He needed a few minutes of distance to catch his breath. He had never had a woman in his cab before, let alone

one who smelled as intoxicating as she did. He didn't know what she bathed in, but it wasn't the lodge's complimentary body wash.

After his nerves had cooled, he tested the ground near Emma's door and cleared the snow off the tracks so she could exit safely. When he climbed up to open her door, he saw she was sound asleep through the window. He didn't have the heart to wake her. In hindsight, he probably should've waited until tomorrow to ask her to come out with them. He had assumed she traveled all night judging by the time she had arrived. Sandy told him she had fallen asleep before dinner. The woman was exhausted and sleeping for two. A fact he needed to keep reminding himself of.

EMMA WOKE TO the sound of Dylan climbing in next to her. The question was, what was he climbing into? Considering she was sitting upright, they weren't in bed together. Although she could have sworn she had been dreaming just that a few minutes ago. She rubbed her eyes and forced herself to open them. Darkness surrounded them.

She reached out in front of her and met the hard steel of the snowcat. "You've got to be kidding me." She attempted to straighten her spine. "Did I fall asleep on your tour?"

"Technically, no. We were already stopped when you fell asleep."

Emma checked her watch and then realized she'd forgotten to put it on today. "How long was I out?"

"Maybe a half hour. I told everyone you decided

to stay inside because it was so cold. This probably wasn't a good idea after the day you've had." Dylan shifted to face her. "You need your sleep. At least you can stay in bed tomorrow." He started the snowcat.

"Not quite. I have a conference call with my boss in the afternoon that I need to prepare for. I don't suppose you could help a girl out and listen to my proposal before then?" Emma hadn't given up hope yet.

Warmth quickly faded from Dylan's face. "I don't think so."

"You know I had to ask."

"I wish you wouldn't. You could have yourself a nice little vacation while we're snowed in if you would just accept that I'm not selling you the ranch."

"And I wish it were that simple. Since we're talking about being snowed in, what happens if a guest has a medical emergency?"

Dylan pushed both control sticks forward as the snowcat began to move. "We've had it happen before. We take the snowcat to the nearest paved road and the ambulance or sheriff's department meets us there. If need be, we can drive this straight to the hospital, but we can't drive it down Main Street at will."

At least there was a way to get to the hospital. Emma shifted uncomfortably in her seat. She wished her daughter would settle down for the night. Then again, she probably sensed the movement despite the snowcat's relatively smooth ride on the freshly fallen snow.

By the time they reached the lodge, the snow had begun falling heavily again. She'd be glad to get back to her room and into bed. She'd start fresh in the morning. And brace herself for the onslaught of her boss.

Dylan hesitated after he helped her out of the snowcat. For a brief moment, she thought he might agree to hear her proposal in the morning.

"Get a good night's sleep. Do you need me to get someone to help you to your room?"

"Um, no. Thank you." So much for wishful thinking. She'd try again in the morning. She'd come too far to give up now.

Chapter Four

Emma showered, dressed and got downstairs by seven the following morning, eager to eat breakfast and try to persuade Dylan to hear her proposal one last time before her conference call. She had glanced out the window earlier but only saw a sea of white through the darkness. That was all she saw last night before she went to bed, too. It was still snowing. She'd only been on the ranch for one day and she was already homesick. It was one thing to travel and have places to go and see. The prospect of being confined on the ranch for the next few days was less exciting than watching water drip from a faucet.

Her stomach grumbled and the scent of fresh baked muffins beckoned her to the dining area. She knew the ranch had a breakfast buffet, but she hadn't expected one this large. And there they were…a basket of glorious golden blueberry muffins. She snatched one before she even picked up a plate. Unable to wait until she sat down, she bit into the streusel-covered top. Heaven couldn't have created a better muffin.

"Oh, my God, French toast!" *Carbs!* Her body

craved them like no tomorrow. She piled four slices on her plate and doused them in real maple syrup. Not the artificial stuff. She would kill for a cup of regular coffee, but settled for a small carton of orange juice, instead. *Sugar!* Her body craved that, too. Her mother would die if she saw what she had eaten over the past twenty-four hours. Emma didn't care. She knew pregnancy wasn't a free pass to eat whatever she wanted, but sometimes you just had to make an exception. She just hoped they didn't bring out pancakes because then somebody would have to roll her out the door.

"Good morning." Sandy greeted her at the table. "I didn't expect to see you up this early. I saw you drooling over the coffee. Would you like a cup of decaf? I brewed a pot a few minutes ago."

"No thank you. It gives me cotton mouth and just makes me crave the real thing that much more." Emma unwrapped her silverware from her napkin and began cutting into her French toast. "Please give my compliments to the chef on those muffins. They are amazing. I haven't tried anything else yet, but I'm sure it will be as good, if not better than it smells."

"You really like the muffins?" Sandy beamed. "I made them. And Melinda made the French toast. I don't know if you met her or not last night. She's another server here." Sandy looked around the room. "She's the tall blonde over by the kitchen door. The one that looks like she should be modeling for *Sports Illustrated* instead of working on a ranch. Rhonda's also on kitchen duty this morning because the staff still couldn't make it in due to the road closures. She's the one with the reddish-purple updo next to Melinda. The chefs don't live on the ranch like we do."

"You made this?" Emma waved her fork. "Did you also make last night's dinner?"

"We sure did. We're all cross-trained here. I love cooking so it's always a treat for me to cook for everyone." Sandy grabbed a heated syrup pitcher from the buffet and set it in front of her. "Here, in case you want some more."

"This is incredible. You should move into the kitchen instead of serving."

"I had planned to, but then Jax said he was selling the ranch." Sandy grimaced. "But now that it's not for sale, I'll have that chance again. Unless you changed Dylan's mind last night."

"No chance of that." Guilt crept into Emma's heart. The woman had dreams and aspirations and she was there to take them away. Wonderful. "Any word on how much snow we had overnight?"

"Eight inches. Not quite the foot they had expected. Normally we don't see this type of accumulation until late January or early February. But it has been known to happen."

"So I guess you're still stuck with me." Emma tried to smile. The snow worked in her favor at the moment, but unless she could change Dylan's mind, she'd go stir-crazy on the ranch.

"We're all in this together. Don't worry. We have plenty of provisions and the lodge has generators in case we lose power. Dylan's brother Harlan is a deputy sheriff in town so he'll keep us updated on the roads." Sandy pulled out a chair next to her and sat down. "You and Dylan looked awfully cozy in the cab of the snowcat when you pulled out of here last night."

Emma wiped at her mouth, no longer hungry. "As cozy as two people can get when the driver has both of his hands full steering a multi-ton vehicle across the snow. Believe me when I tell you, Dylan has no plans to sell this place. He won't even discuss it."

"I already knew that. I thought maybe there was a romance brewing between you two."

She pushed her plate aside. "You are out of your mind. Don't take this the wrong way, but this lifestyle isn't for me. I'm used to having every amenity available at a moment's notice. We have road closures, but never like this. At least not where I live in Chicago. I'm blocks away from the hospital so they clear those roads first. This is very—"

"Calming, if you allow it to be."

Emma covered her mouth for fear she might burst out laughing. The Montana wilderness was not calming to her. It was terrifying in more than one way.

"Maybe he'll take you out for a private sleigh ride today." Sandy nibbled her bottom lip. "Can you just imagine?"

Emma had never been the hopeless-romantic type. Even romantic was questionable. She'd read the fairy tales and had hoped her Prince Charming would sweep her off her feet one day. Then she had gotten knocked up and her boyfriend walked out on her. So much for romance. And hopeless? Yeah, she was feeling pretty hopeless right now, considering she couldn't even convince Dylan to listen to her.

"I think you're super excited about your wedding and you're trying to play matchmaker. You're conveniently forgetting I'm carrying another man's baby."

"But I overheard you tell Dylan that he wasn't in your life."

"That's right, he's not."

"Then what's the problem? Dylan loves kids. He still misses the ones he lost when Lauren divorced him. And you challenge each other."

"How do you know that?" Emma jabbed her fork into a piece of French toast. It would be a shame to let it go to waste. "I've only been here for a day."

"I see the way you look at each other. And the way he sang to you last night." Sandy fanned herself with her hand. "Now that was hot."

"It was a Christmas song, not a love song," Emma protested.

"But you were standing under the mistletoe."

"An unfortunate misstep on my part. It's not like he came over and kissed me afterward."

"And what if I had?" Dylan said from behind her.

Emma froze. Mouth-open, fork-in-hand, syrup-dripping froze. Now, she was going to die.

DYLAN KNEW HE wasn't playing fair. Then again, Emma hadn't played fair since the day they had met.

"I'll give you two a little privacy." Sandy stood and held out her chair for him.

Before he even had a chance to sit, Emma rose. "I should be going, too."

"Going where? The ranch is snowed in."

Emma's pinky grazed his. It was innocent and intimate in the same breath. And dammit if it hadn't left him wanting more. He moved his chair a few inches farther away from hers before he sat down.

"Did you change your mind about hearing my proposal?"

"No." He shook his head. "But I would like to pick your brain"

Emma's eyes widened. "About the ranch? Dylan, I have a conference call this afternoon and I have to explain how I can't convince you to give me a few hours of your time. Yet, you want to pick my brain, as you put it, over the ranch. Yeah, um, I'm sorry. That's not going to happen."

"You seem to be awfully stressed over one phone call. Stay and have breakfast with me. I insist." Dylan picked up her dish. "Let me get you a hot plate of food. You can meet some of my people and relax for an hour."

"No offense, but being near you is anything but relaxing. Especially when you're pushing your own agenda."

"I haven't asked much of you, but you're asking me to give up my entire life. Honestly, I didn't think having breakfast with me and my employees was that big of a deal." Dylan forced himself to remain polite. "Don't worry, they won't tell you their life stories. I just thought it would be nice if you met some of Silver Bells' extended family. The ranch wasn't just my uncle. It's all of us together."

"Okay." Emma sat down. "I'll stay."

"Oh-kay." The way she agreed with him seemed off. He half-expected her to bolt before he returned to the table. "I'll be right back."

By the time he reached the buffet, many of the guests were in line ahead of him. When the ranch had been fully operational, they'd had a separate employee buffet two hours earlier. They had combined them when there wasn't enough of either group for a full buffet. At least it made the massive dining room appear much less empty.

He checked the table a few times to make sure Emma was still there. She had her head buried in that phone of hers. A part of him wished the snowstorm would take out the internet, but then he wouldn't be able to make his own inquiries to save the ranch. He'd spent half the night online researching potential investors. He'd even sent out a few feeler emails, but this wasn't his forte.

With Christmas less than a week away, he figured most people wouldn't want to be bothered discussing a business deal this size. He wondered if one partner would even be enough. He might need to form his own investment group. But who would want to finance a sinking ship?

Dylan stopped a few of his ranch hands' wives in line and directed them to the large round table where Emma sat. By the time he arrived, it was almost full and she was happily chatting about babies. Perfect.

She was forming a connection with them. That was exactly what he had hoped for.

"The women want to teach me how to knit." Emma frowned as he placed a fresh plate in front of her and took a seat.

"What's wrong with knitting?" Most of the women he knew did it. Wasn't that the in thing? Not that he was up-to-date on women's hobbies but, based on bits of conversations he'd overheard around the ranch, many of his female employees were involved in some sort of crafting.

"I can barely sew a button on a shirt, let alone intricately weave yarn into clothing."

"So make a simple blanket. Create something special for your daughter that she'll hand down to her own daughter someday."

"I hadn't expected you to be the sentimental type."

"I'm sentimental about a lot of things." Dylan forked a mouthful of scrambled eggs.

"I know, I know. This ranch being one of them."

"I'm attached to this ranch because I live on it and my employees depend on it. But I wouldn't say it's a sentimental attachment. The homestead my family lost after my father died…that was a sentimental attachment. I hope to one day buy it back if the current owner ever decides to sell."

"I'm sorry, I didn't know."

"No need to apologize. It's no secret around here. My brother Ryder killed my father. He was sentenced to ten years in prison, half of which he's already served. I'm the oldest of five. I've always looked after everyone else. I feel the responsibility to have a place where people can work and make an honest living. I wanted Ryder to have that option once he got out of jail—if there's anything left to salvage of our relationship—but now that may not be possible if the ranch continues on a downward spiral."

"And you want me to help you?"

Dylan nodded. "You've met some of these people. This isn't just my home. It's theirs, too. I don't want them to have to start over. I could handle it. Many of them can't."

Emma looked down at her hands. "I didn't realize how difficult this has been for you."

Her eyes met his and for the first time, he believed her. "No, you didn't."

Emma tensed. "At least we have that much in common. I don't think you understand how difficult this has been for me, either."

As much as he could use Emma's expertise on how to entice potential investors, asking her to do so would violate her ethics. It was a shame they had such opposite goals. Their combined determination would have made them a great team.

It was nine o'clock before Emma waddled away from the table. Somewhere during that time, she had amassed the phone numbers of ranch women willing to share all the secrets of child-rearing, or so they said. Melinda had a six-month-old of her own and had generously offered to teach her the basics of bathing and changing an infant. Emma wasn't sure she was

ready for the hands-on approach just yet. She still had
the child-care class to take at the hospital back home.
She had thought she would have two more months to
prepare for actual infant holding. The thought terrified her more and more each day. Especially since
she had never held a baby…ever.

When noon rolled around—one o'clock Chicago
time—Emma's stomach began to churn. Either the
baby was pressing her nausea button or her nerves
about the conference call were getting the best of her.
She was halfway to her room when her phone rang.

Crap! It was a video call. Not what she had expected.

"Hello."

"Emma." Charlie's face appeared on the screen.
"I'm here with Rob and Don. We need an update on
the Silver Bells acquisition."

"I haven't made any progress yet. I—"

"You've been there for a day and you've done nothing?" Charlie scowled.

"The ranch is snowed in and Dylan's had his
hands full dealing with that. I've barely seen him,"
she fibbed. "I'm sure I'll have a chance once things
calm down around here."

Emma sat on a bench in the hallway, dreading
Charlie's response.

"Okay, getting snowed in may be a good thing."
Don's face popped into the screen. "That will give
you some time to work on…" He shuffled some papers. "Dylan, is it?"

"Yes." She'd just said his name two seconds ago. So much for her home team being on top of things.

Charlie's brows furrowed. "Emma, are you sure you can handle this?"

"You need to find something to use against this Dylan person," Rob said before she had a chance to respond to Charlie. "Convince him to sell at any cost."

Emma fought the retort that was on the tip of her tongue. She refused to play dirty.

"I don't need to remind you what's at stake, do I?" Charlie leaned in, his face filled the entire screen like an ominous presence. "If you can't close this deal then I'm afraid you're not ready for the acquisitions director promotion. Why don't I send Don up to assist you?"

Emma couldn't believe what she was hearing. She didn't need Don's help. "The roads are closed. You can't get here. Nobody can get here."

"I'm sure somebody around there must rent snowmobiles," Don snipped.

Snowmobiles. Of course, he would think of that. "I'm sure they do. But thanks, anyway. I'm fine on my own."

"Emma, close this deal before you leave there. We have too many long-standing investors counting on this."

Emma stood and felt lightheaded. She gripped the corner of the wall and sat down. "I'm trying, Charlie. Believe me, I'm evaluating every available option."

"Okay, then. We'll talk more later. Take care of that baby of yours." And then the screen went blank.

"Merry Christmas to you, as— Dylan! How long have you been standing there?"

Mr. Pick-Your-Brain leaned languidly against the wall opposite her.

"Long enough to see that conversation made your blood boil."

"You know it's not nice to eavesdrop."

"You're having a conference call in the middle of the hallway in my lodge. It's kind of impossible not to overhear."

Yeah, okay that was true. For some reason, face-to-face conference calls with men in her hotel room creeped her out. "Now you understand my pressure?"

"Let me ask you something." Dylan settled next to her on the bench, the length of his thigh touching hers. "Why do you put up with it? Can't you find another job where they appreciate your talents? That was a whole lot of ridicule for a short conversation."

"Then I would be admitting defeat." Emma wouldn't dream of quitting her job. Not after the six years of her life she'd devoted to the commercial real estate acquisitions firm. "It was the first place I worked for when I got out of college. I literally started at the bottom as an intern and worked my way up. I've accomplished quite a bit for someone who's only twenty-eight. My goal was to make acquisitions director before I turned thirty. The problem is, that position rarely opens. The last acquisitions director had been there for twenty years. It's available because he retired. This is my chance. Probably my only chance to advance."

"But I'm not willing to sell."

"I know but—" Emma doubled forward. The pain below her ribs felt like someone had shoved an ice pick through her body. "Dylan, help me! Something's wrong with my baby. Oh, God, please!"

Chapter Five

The urgency in her voice told him something was really wrong. He lifted her into his arms. "I've got you." Dylan carried her down the stairs and into the lobby. "Sandy!" he shouted toward the dining room. "I need to get Emma to the hospital. Stay with her while I get the snowcat."

"Oh, my God, it hurts." Emma sobbed as he lowered her into the lobby chair. "Please hurry, Dylan. Don't let me lose my baby."

"I won't." He promised as he ran out the front door. He pulled his keys from his pocket and jumped on his snowmobile. His hands shook as he found the right key. Jamming it into the ignition, he started the machine and tore off toward the stables. From a distance he could see the layer of snow on the snowcat's windshield and he prayed it hadn't iced over. There wasn't time to wait for it to defrost.

The snowmobile skidded to a stop alongside the snowcat's tracks. He snatched the keys from the ignition and fumbled for the one to open the door. Then he hopped onto the track and swiped at the windshield. It was all powder, thank God. He unlocked the door, swung it wide and climbed into the driver's seat. The diesel turned over without hesitation. His snowcat may be old, but it was reliable.

When he reached the lodge's entrance, he couldn't be sure how much time had passed. One second seemed too long. He felt something had been off with Emma since she had arrived and his instincts had been correct.

Dylan parked outside the entrance and raced inside for her. Tears streamed down her face as he lifted her back into his arms. He tightened his grip on her and stepped into the cold. A bitter wind stung his cheeks as he tucked her closer to his body.

Sandy ran ahead of them and opened the passenger door. "Here's her bag. Rhonda went to her room and got it. And I called Harlan," she panted. "He's going to meet you at the intersection of South Fork and Anderson. He said the roads to the hospital are plowed from there."

"Thank you." He eased Emma onto the seat and gently fastened her seat belt across her lap. "The hospital isn't far." He closed the door, looked skyward and silently prayed Jax was looking down on them.

DYLAN PACED THE hospital waiting area. A wiser man would have dropped Emma off and been done with the situation. Unfortunately, he had this inexplicable need to remain close by in case she needed him, even though the logical part of his brain reassured him she wouldn't. Sure, he wanted to be certain she was all right, but he had zero connection to this woman and her child outside of their nonexistent sale of the ranch.

Okay, so that wasn't altogether true. He'd been physically attracted to Emma from the moment they'd met. He just had a strong distaste for her endgame. But his attraction to her began and ended there. There certainly wasn't an emotional attachment. Yet he couldn't force himself to walk out the hospital's doors.

"Mr. Sheridan." A nurse in bright pink scrubs approached him. "Both momma and baby are stable. The doctor is about to begin the ultrasound, so if you will follow me, I will take you to her."

Mr. Sheridan? The woman assumed he was Emma's husband. He opened his mouth to correct her but ended up saying the opposite of what he'd intended. "Great, thank you."

The walk down the hospital corridor seemed endless. With each step, the voice inside his head begged him to run in the opposite direction. But his body refused to obey. He needed to see for himself that Emma and the baby were fine.

He halted in the doorway of the room when he saw her reclined on a bed, wearing a hiked-up hospital gown to expose her bare belly and nothing more than a sheet covering her lap and legs. Two wide bands stretched around her abdomen and held what Dylan assumed were fetal monitors of some sort in place. Emma's attention was transfixed on the screen attached to her stomach as the sound of a heartbeat reverberated throughout the otherwise quiet room.

"Your daughter still sounds strong and healthy."

The doctor looked up from the monitor's printout. "Your blood pressure is my primary concern. It's more elevated than I would prefer." The woman glanced in his direction. "Is this the baby's father?" she asked.

Emma held out her hand to him. "Please, come in." Despite her weak smile, fear emanated from her delicate features. Even if he wanted to, he couldn't leave now. Any desire to escape had faded and he didn't understand why. He crossed the room to her bed. Her fingers entwined with his, gripping his hand tightly. "Dylan's a friend," she said as her eyes met his. "Right? At least for today."

They had been sworn enemies since the beginning, but even he refused to deny her when she needed someone most. He scanned the numerous machines connected to her body. "Are you in labor?"

She squeezed her eyes shut and dug her fingers into his flesh as the doctor returned her attention to the printout. "Easy, Emma, it's almost over. She's experiencing Braxton-Hicks contractions. It's false labor, but we'll continue to monitor her overnight. Let's begin your ultrasound."

"I should leave." As soon as he uttered the words, he realized he hadn't meant them. He didn't know if it was because he wanted to see for himself that the baby was okay or if his strong desire to stay was out of curiosity. He'd never been involved in any pregnancy aside from his brother Harlan's wife, Belle, who was almost in the middle of her second trimester. He'd seen an ultrasound photo, but that was the extent of it. When she didn't release his hand after the contraction subsided, it unnerved him even more. The ultrasound didn't scare him. The situation did. He didn't want to get close to Emma or her baby, because he had no intention of ever forming an attachment to another man's kid again. Losing his stepchildren had almost destroyed him and he refused to be a two-time fool.

Emma averted her eyes. "I want you to stay." Her voice no more than a whisper.

"Okay." Dylan relented. He reached for the chair near the bed and pulled it closer.

"This will feel cold at first." The doctor squeezed a tube of clear gel on Emma's abdomen and spread it with the ultrasound probe. Various shades of white and grey danced across the screen until an image of the baby appeared. "There's your daughter."

"My little butter bean." Emma smiled through her tears. "Is she really all right?"

The doctor continued to move the probe. "I don't see any abnormalities. She's exactly where she should be at thirty-two weeks."

Dylan fought the urge to wipe away her tears. He looked from the screen to Emma's belly and back again. That tiny person was growing inside of her. He'd seen plenty of horse ultrasounds, but this was different. This was…far too intimate for her to share with him. She needed her mother or her best friends by her side. Not someone who hadn't been very nice to her.

"We'll perform another one tomorrow, but I'm fairly confident there won't be any change. I'm more concerned about your blood pressure and the possibility of preeclampsia. Your baby is healthy and strong, and I need you to be healthy and strong so you can carry her at least another six weeks." She handed the probe to another woman in pink. "Tricia is going to get a good ultrasound photo for you. I want you to rest tonight. I know that's difficult to do in a hospital. We'll leave your fetal monitors on as a precaution, so if there's anything out of the ordinary they will alert us right away. Again, Emma, the signs point to Braxton-Hicks and not preterm labor. Try to get some sleep and I'll check on you in the morning." The doctor squeezed her other hand.

"Thank you," Emma said as the woman left the room. She readjusted her gown and pressed the bed's remote until she sat more upright. "And thank you for staying here with me even though you didn't have to." She smiled up at Dylan. "I didn't want to go through this alone."

"Don't mention it." Dylan stood, breaking physical contact with Emma. He jammed his hands in his pockets to prevent touching her again. "I should get going and let you sleep."

"As if I could sleep now. Besides, it's not even two o'clock." She stared at the photo Tricia handed her. "Believe me, I am anything but tired. Stay with me for a little while longer. Help distract my mind from all of this."

Two o'clock? One hour had felt like twelve. "What would you like to talk about?" He didn't know how to idly chitchat with a pregnant woman. He sat on the edge of the chair, braced for a quick exit. He'd already crossed too many lines this evening. "Baby names? You mentioned earlier that you haven't chosen one yet. Do you have any in mind?" Dylan couldn't believe what he was saying. He sounded like his mother. Now, there was a woman who would have been right at home discussing babies with Emma. If only she hadn't moved to California, he could have called and asked her to trade places with him. For both his and Emma's sake.

"I haven't even had a chance to buy a baby name book yet." A tinge of pink rose to her cheeks. "I've been busting my butt to close this deal before I go on maternity leave."

"There is no deal, Emma. I know the ranch is in trouble, but I'll find a way to save it. Selling is not an option. Your vision for it doesn't mesh with mine."

"Can you hand me my bag over there?"

Dylan retrieved the large leather purse from the windowsill. Emma dug inside of it and removed a small black tablet. "Let me show you my plans for Silver Bells."

"You have got to be kidding me. You're in the hospital, supposedly concerned about your baby and you're still trying to convince me to sell. No wonder your blood pressure is so high. Instead of fixating on my ranch, you should download a baby name book on that thing." Dylan returned the chair he had been sitting on to its original place against the wall. "I think it's time for me to call it a night."

"I am concerned about my baby. That's why I came to Montana."

"That doesn't make any sense."

"Once I have this baby, I won't be able to travel for work any longer. I can't afford a nanny to fly around the world with me. My job pays for my expenses only. Not a companion's. I don't have a husband or anyone else at home to leave my child with while I go on business trips. Besides, I plan to nurse my daughter. I can't be gone twenty days a month and do that. I'm on my own. I shouldn't even be telling you any of this, but maybe you'll understand if I do." Emma took a deep breath before continuing. "The promotion I told you about earlier isn't something I want. It's something I need. Without it, I'll have to accept a lesser position. Living in Chicago is expensive enough. Even more so when you're a single mom. I need to secure my child's future and the only way I can do that is to convince you to sell. You only heard the initial proposal. Your uncle changed a lot of things. He told me you wouldn't give him the time of day when it came to discussing the plans. At least look at our final design. You might be surprised."

"I'm sorry. I sympathize with your situation, but I can't put your job security above my employees. Including myself. Regardless of what your plan is, you've already said there are no guarantees you would rehire my employees and even if there were, they would be out of work for months. That alone is why I won't hear you out. Change those parameters and then maybe I'd be willing to listen. But you're still asking me to give up a part of my family. Silver Bells was my uncle's ranch. A place I found a hell of a lot of serenity in during some really dark times."

"Your uncle was willing to give it up. And I'm sorry, but there is no way I can promise to take on a full staff while they're renovating the ranch. It doesn't fit into the timetable."

"Then you don't fit into mine. I'm sorry, Emma." Dylan noticed her blood pressure had increased since the doctor had left the room. "I'll return in the morning to see how you're doing. I wish you would take the doctor's advice and relax for the rest of the day. I don't know what the relationship is between you and your family, but maybe you should call them. Or a friend, at least. Let business rest for a while. I'll see you tomorrow."

Dylan awkwardly waved as he beelined for the door. Once out in the hallway, he questioned if he'd been too hard on her. He resisted the urge to peek back in her room to make sure she was okay. He'd already gotten far too involved. The gnawing at the pit of his stomach told him this was just the beginning.

EMMA STARED AT the doorway, willing Dylan to return. She hadn't meant to run him off. While it was true she wanted to talk business, the truth was she didn't want to be alone. And while she needed to acquire the ranch to secure her promotion, Silver Bells happened to be the only subject they had in common.

Great job, Emma. You managed to run off another man. Not that Dylan Slade was of any consequence.

Well, at least not outside of work. Although, if Paul had been half as attentive as Dylan had been today, they might still be together. She knew very little about his personal life, but Jax had made a point to mention on more than one occasion that Dylan was single. If he was as stubborn about everything else in his life as he was about the sale of the ranch, she could understand why. Regardless, the fact he had remained by her side spoke volumes to his integrity. She wouldn't mind a man like that in her life. She could do without the orneriness, though.

Emma wanted to remain calm, but the constant flutter in her belly made it impossible. Never mind the glare of the fetal monitor screen, the repeated squeeze of the blood-pressure cuff, the annoying pulse oximeter at the end of her finger and the two bands wrapped around her belly. They were constant reminders that things were not okay. While her pregnancy had been a surprise, she had adjusted rather quickly to the idea of being a mom despite her ex-good-for-nothing walking out on her.

She wanted to give her daughter the love and attention she hadn't received growing up. As far as her parents were concerned, she was surprised they had found time to conceive a child since they sure hadn't had time to raise one. Not that she'd had a difficult life, because hers had been rather charmed. At least from the outside looking in.

Nannies had raised her until she went away to boarding school. She'd traveled the world on vacations and had even spent a semester at sea aboard a luxury cruise liner. But there was a price for being away from home most of her childhood. She never felt a bond with her parents. Her baby wasn't even born and she felt more of a bond with her daughter than she'd ever felt with her own mother. When she had spent time with them, they'd been far from affectionate. She had received more attention from her nannies and she refused to ever play a secondary role to a stand-in mom.

Her mother was an appellate court judge and her father was a neurosurgeon. Their work tended to come above needless hugs or petty playtime. They had groomed Emma to succeed, and she craved that success. But only so she could become a hands-on mother and be able to make enough money to raise her daughter more conventionally.

Emma pulled her phone from her bag and scrolled through the contacts. She hadn't even told her parents she was going to Montana. Not that they expected her to keep them apprised of her travel schedule. She tapped the screen and waited for them to answer. After the fifth ring, she just about gave up when she heard her mother's voice.

"Hi, Mom. I just wanted to let you know I'm in the hospital."

"You're having the baby?" Kate Sheridan asked. "Is it that time already?"

Emma sighed. She envied the women whose mothers had their due date circled on the calendar and counted down week by week with them. "Hopefully not for another eight weeks. The doctor will be happy with six, though. I'm in Montana on business and I started having contractions. Turns out they were only Braxton-Hicks, but they're keeping me in the hospital overnight because my blood pressure is elevated. They want to rule out preeclampsia."

"You're keeping your weight down, aren't you?" Kate asked. Her mother was obsessed with other people's weight. They could be the most beautiful people in the world, but heaven forbid they carried an extra five pounds. Her mother always had to point it out.

"I'm doing fine. Thank you for asking, though." Emma huffed. "And yes, I'm keeping my weight down." As long as she didn't count the food she'd eaten in the last twenty-four hours.

"Emma, if you called to argue, I don't have time for it."

"I thought you would be concerned." The hint of a contraction warned her to remain calm. "My mistake."

"You had some false labor pains. It's common. I'm glad you're okay, but it's nothing to get upset over. I'm assuming you're there to wrap up that ranch deal."

Emma exhaled slowly. "I'm trying to, but the owner doesn't want to sell."

"I don't know what you're going to do, then. You need this promotion."

"I will figure it out." She ground her back teeth together.

"I'm sure you will. You always do. You're a strong woman, Emma. Don't forget that."

Amazingly enough, when Emma had found out she

was pregnant, her parents hadn't gotten upset. She'd expected them to chastise her, but they said they had faith in her ability to raise a child without a partner to lean on. They also made it clear that their parents hadn't helped them and they expected her to stand on her own if she was determined to keep her child. At least her mother thought she was strong, because today she felt anything but.

"Thank you, Mom. I have some notes to review since I can't do much of anything else right now. I will give you a call if anything changes. I should be released tomorrow."

"Okay. Get to work."

"Bye, Mom."

Emma rested her head against the pillow and closed her eyes. She didn't know what she had expected from that conversation, but some concern or comforting words would have been nice. Another twinge from deep within her body jolted her upright. She quickly checked the numerous screens next to the bed, not exactly sure what she was looking for. No bells and alarms went off. That was a good sign. The cuff around her arm tightened. She checked the monitor over her left shoulder. 135/80. It wasn't great but it was still better than the 140/90 it had read when she was admitted.

"Easy, butter bean." She needed to choose a name for her daughter. Calling her a vegetable, however sweetly intended, no longer felt right. She didn't even have a birthing plan. Or a crib. Or a car seat. Or anything. She kept meaning to sign up for the prepared childbirth and infant care classes the hospital offered in Chicago but hadn't found the time yet. Jennie had offered to go with her for support. Considering they only held the classes once a month, she needed to make it a priority.

Emma opened the web browser on her tablet and registered for the next available classes. Her first and second Saturdays of the new year were officially booked. At least she felt she'd accomplished something for her daughter.

She pressed the call button and asked for something to drink. The doctor said her baby was strong and healthy, and she intended to keep her that way. If that meant temporary bed rest then so be it. It would give her the opportunity to reformulate her plan of attack on Dylan Slade. She needed to find a way to make things work for them both. She couldn't give him what he wanted. She couldn't guarantee jobs and she couldn't promise employment for the next six months.

Her decisions affected many people regardless of what she did or didn't do. In the end, some people would lose their jobs. There was no avoiding it. It weighed on her conscience with each acquisition, but it was business and she couldn't allow her personal feelings to get in the way.

Chapter Six

"You've got to be kidding me." It was two in the morning and Dylan added another outstanding invoice to the growing mound beside him. Sleep had evaded him as he pored over the ranch's financial records in his uncle's office. He'd uncovered more debts Jax had hidden from him. Maybe hidden wasn't fair. But they were debts Dylan hadn't known about. "What are you doing to me Jax?"

His uncle had handled most of the business affairs while he oversaw the management and maintenance of the many ranch buildings, including the lodge, private guest cabins and stables, along with the ranch's 730 acres and almost a hundred horses.

Dylan had gone to the lodge office to get Emma out of his head. He thought if he searched hard enough, he'd uncover an overlooked bank account or discover some way to keep the ranch and send her packing. The farther she was from him, the better. His heart had grown restless ever since she stepped foot on Silver Bells putting him in a dangerous and vulnerable position. And those were two words he refused to entertain.

The increased debt meant the money he had in savings wouldn't carry the ranch for as long as he'd anticipated. He was in more trouble than he thought. There had to be a way out. He just hadn't found it yet. He sighed heavily and removed another unmarked folder from one of many file boxes next to the desk. It was either this or call everyone they'd done business with over the years and ask if the ranch owed them money. At this point, he didn't know which would be easier.

By the time Dylan entered the stables later that morning, he had already downed two pots of coffee and was no closer to a solution.

Regardless of how many times he said he wouldn't sell Emma's company the ranch, if he didn't come up with alternative financing soon, he feared he would have to sell to someone. But it wouldn't be Emma. They wanted to destroy the place he loved.

Garrett and his two kids were visiting for Christmas and Dylan debated about asking his brother one more time if he'd consider buying into the ranch. He'd asked him a year ago, when Jax first started his rumblings about selling the ranch, but Garrett said he didn't want to uproot the kids. It had been almost three years since his sister-in-law Rebecca had died from cancer and his brother had thrown himself into managing her parents' cattle ranch in Wyoming.

Every time they spoke on the phone, Garrett sounded wearier of living under their roof. He had said numerous times he felt like they were living in a constant state of depression. Maybe he'd reconsider this time. The only thing stopping Dylan was his conscience. Did he really want to be responsible for his brother sinking his savings into a ranch that may not turn around when he had two kids to support?

"Hey, man," Wes said from behind Dylan's desk as he entered his office. "I expected you here an hour ago."

"And I expected you not to show up for work again." Dylan crossed the room and hitched his thumb signaling for Wes to get up. "I was at the lodge going through Jax's less-than-stellar filing system."

"Find anything to help you?" Wes grabbed his coffee and a notepad before standing.

"Nope." Dylan rubbed his morning stubble. He should shave before visiting Emma at the hospital. Then again, it wasn't like he had to impress her. "What are you working on?" Dylan angled his head to read the notes tucked under Wes's arm as he walked by.

"Just working out some dates." Wes pushed up his hat. "A rodeo school in Ramblewood, Texas, offered me a teaching position during my last competition. I called them yesterday and accepted. I'm going to head down there on the second. The job will still allow me to compete and I'll be doing what I love most. Bull riding."

"That soon, huh?" Dylan hated losing another employee, not that Wes was around much. But even more so, he hated losing his brother. "It sounds like a great opportunity, but are you sure this is what you want?"

"Staying is too hard." Wes shook his head. "Even harder now that Jax is gone. There are too many reminders here. Every time I drive into town I keep thinking I see Dad's truck or Mom coming out of a store. It's been five years and I still hear people talking behind my back about Ryder. Garrett had the right idea. He got far away from Saddle Ridge. I need that clean break. I want to spend one last Christmas with you guys, and then I'm out."

His brother's words felt like a fist to the gut. "One last Christmas? You're not planning to come home ever again?"

"Don't you get it?" Deep lines creased Wes's forehead. "Saddle Ridge isn't home anymore. Ryder destroyed that. I have tried, Lord help me, I've tried, but I can't do this anymore. I need to be some place where every corner doesn't hold a memory of what once was. I'm tired of looking backwards."

"Yeah, I get it." Out of the five brothers, Wes had taken their father's death the hardest, not counting the guilt Ryder had to live with. "If you ever change your mind, the door here is always open."

Wes laughed under his breath. "Providing you still have a door to keep open."

"Ain't that the truth." Dylan sat down behind his desk. "If you can think of any potential investors, let me know. I'd ask you, but I already know the answer."

"Sell."

"What?"

Wes took the last swig of his coffee and tossed the cup in the trash. "Sell this place and start over someplace else. Come to Texas with me. You can do this same thing down there, only without the snow."

"I can't give up."

"You can't or you won't?" Wes strode to the office door. "Just remember, wherever I am, my door's always open, too."

Dylan leaned back in his chair and pinched the bridge of his nose. He wished letting go was as easy for him as it was for Wes. It would make his life a hell of a lot easier.

Two HOURS LATER, Dylan arrived at the hospital to check on Emma. She'd been at the forefront of his mind all morning. Despite their temporary truce, he needed to continually remind himself who he was dealing with. The woman wanted to destroy the place that had become his sanctuary. The Silver Bells Ranch wasn't intended to be a five-star couples-only luxury resort with yoga and mud baths. The only mud you'd find here was on the bottom of your boots and chances were it wasn't mud. His ranch was a chuck wagon, line dancing, horse-riding-in-the-Montana-mountains experience. That's what people wanted. At least, they had until other guest ranches had cropped up in the Saddle Ridge area. Now Silver Bells had to compete with the new. He needed to find a way to keep the ranch open without going further in debt. Time was ticking down and all income would officially end in two weeks. If the ranch went under that meant the last five years of his life had been for naught.

He had lost everything he loved most when he invested in the ranch and had devoted every waking hour since to forget Lauren and the kids. He had succeeded up until now. Emma's presence reminded him how much he still wanted a family. At thirty-five, his chances grew slimmer each day. Especially when he didn't have the time to meet someone or go out on a date.

He envied the families Garrett and Harlan had created. Granted, he wasn't the only Slade sibling without kids. His brother Wes was adamantly against them while his other brother Ryder still had five and a half years left on his ten-year prison sentence.

"I have to be able to travel." Dylan heard Emma say as he approached her hospital room. "Once I wrap up my business here, I have a job to get back to. I can't stay in Montana until New Year's Day. You just mean I can't fly, right?"

"No travel at all. Definitely no planes from this point forward. Trains are too dangerous because medical care isn't immediately available if you need it. The same with driving, although the likelihood of a hospital being close by is greater. I don't want you in a seated position for that long. Light exercise is the best thing for you. I will give you a list of what you can and can't do. I'm releasing you from the hospital, but you're not out of the woods yet. Providing there are no further issues during the next two weeks, the train would be your safest bet because you can get up and move around. But not now."

Dylan removed his hat and raked his hand through his hair. He couldn't handle Emma on his ranch for another two weeks. She'd drive him insane.

He cleared his throat loudly to announce his presence before entering the room. "How's the patient this morning?" He didn't want to let on he had overheard their conversation. "You look better." Her color had returned to a delicate pink porcelain compared to the borderline red she had exhibited yesterday. Her blood pressure monitor registered 125/80. Definite improvement there.

"The doctor just told me I can't travel for two weeks." A nurse unfastened one of Emma's belly bands.

Dylan swallowed hard. "Um, is that really necessary?"

The doctor's eyes narrowed at his question. "For the sake of my patient and her unborn child, yes. Yes, it is." She redirected her attention to Emma. "You can choose to do what you want, but I strongly advise you to stay put. Your contractions went on longer than we had anticipated last night. We received your records from your obstetrician in Chicago. After conferring with him, we feel it's best if you stay where I can monitor you closely. I'll get your discharge papers ready and I'll be in to see you before you leave."

"I don't know what I'm going to do." Emma shifted so the nurse could remove the second belly band and fetal monitor. "This was only supposed to be a two-

or three-day trip. My doctor told me I could fly up to thirty-four weeks. So much for that."

Dylan's mind raced in a million directions. As much as he didn't want to get involved, he couldn't possibly turn her out in the cold with only six days until Christmas.

"You're welcome to stay at the ranch for as long as you need."

"I appreciate that. I promise not to be too much trouble."

Dylan wasn't so sure about that. "No more arguing with me over the ranch, though. It just upsets both of us."

The nurse stopped unhooking Emma from her various monitors and regarded him briefly before continuing. Dylan had tried to sound as sympathetic yet firm as possible without coming across as an insensitive jerk. Apparently, he failed at sensitivity.

Emma mumbled a halfhearted okay before easing out of the opposite side of the bed. Dylan averted his eyes just as she realized he had been privy to her pink cotton-clad bottom thanks to the open-backed gown. He had to hand it to her…she was in fine shape at eight months pregnant.

She gripped at her gown. "I can't wait to get into my own clothes. Make that a change of clothes." She grabbed the sweater and leggings she had worn yesterday from a chair and padded toward the bathroom in her thin hospital slippers. "I'll be out in a minute." She began to close the door and then hesitated. "Are the roads open or did you take the snowcat halfway here again?"

"They're open."

"Then would you mind giving me a ride to the ranch?"

"You don't even have to ask."

"Thank you." She smiled sweetly before closing the door. Now that was a smile he could get used to. Not that he wanted to get used to her smile, because Emma wasn't going to be in town long enough for him to get attached to it. She was there for two weeks only.

"I'm going to run down to the cafeteria," Dylan said to the nurse. "That should give her time to do what she needs to do before we go home. I mean back to the ranch. We don't live together."

Dylan groaned. He couldn't escape the room fast enough. He half walked, half ran down the corridor, desperate to distance himself from all things Emma. *Two weeks.* He didn't know how he'd survive two weeks and the holidays near her every day. Sure, he could make a point of avoiding her, but even he wasn't that heartless. Maybe he could convince his sister-in-law, Belle, to spend some time with Emma. They could talk babies and pregnancy.

Dylan's mind was racing by the time he reached the cafeteria. He wanted Emma and her baby off his ranch, but the image of the ultrasound had been burned in his brain. Scared as she may be, Emma was far from weak. He had a suspicion she just hadn't realized her own strength. It wasn't his job to point it out or steer her in the right direction. And it certainly wasn't his place to build her daughter a rocking horse, yet he had found himself sketching one repeatedly on his notepad last night. He'd taken up woodworking in high school and had always found the hobby relaxing. He hadn't thought of building anything child-related since Lauren had packed up her kids and left.

He poured a cup of coffee and sighed. The next two weeks couldn't go by fast enough.

CLIMBING INTO THE passenger side of Dylan's lifted pickup truck was no easy feat in her condition, even with Dylan's assistance. Emma wasn't a big fan of lifted trucks, or any truck for that matter. What was it about boys and their toys? She couldn't even fathom getting a child fastened in a car seat in one of these contraptions. But then, she guessed that was the point. What man wanted to be bothered toting an infant around town? Sure, it looked well and good on television, but most of the men she worked with drove sports cars they had purchased with their yearly bonuses and she guaranteed they were car-seat free. They were in a league she had worked hard to join for the last six years. Unless she closed this deal, it would be forever out of her reach. But how could she convince Dylan to see things her way when he had refused to discuss it further?

"She's only eighteen weeks along, but I'm sure she'd love to get together with you."

"Huh?" Emma stared at him.

"You didn't hear a word I said, did you?"

"No, I'm sorry. My mind was…elsewhere."

"I was talking about my sister-in-law, Belle. She's eighteen weeks pregnant and I'm sure she would love to meet you." Dylan steered the truck out of the hospital parking lot. "She and Harlan live on the other side of town. Maybe we can even go over there if you're up to it. She runs an animal rescue center if you're into that sort of thing."

"Like a dog shelter?"

"No like a farm animal sanctuary. She takes in animals that were injured or born with deformities. Some have suffered ill-treatment or have been rescued from backyard butchers. Any animal in need of a safe forever home can live out their life at Belle's Forever Ranch. They even have a cow named Cash—after Johnny Cash—who will be fitted with a prosthesis shortly, since he had a lower leg amputation this past summer. She does have a few Great Pyrenees watchdogs, though. They protect the center from predators."

"I didn't know places like that existed."

"You need to get out of the city more."

"I will have you know I've traveled the world over numerous times. It's just that most of my destinations are—how should I phrase it—a little more exclusive." Dylan winced at her description and she immediately regretted her poor choice of words. "Not that Saddle Ridge isn't exclusive."

"No, I get it. Saddle Ridge is a small town. So, I have to ask, why are you so interested in my property when places like Aspen and Lake Tahoe fit the lifestyle you're promoting?"

"Price and acreage for one. Saddle Ridge has the same outdoor attractions the well-known resort areas have. We've been looking to acquire a large ranch away from the usual travel destinations but not completely off the beaten path. We want to take full advantage of northwestern Montana's year-round activities without sacrificing an ounce of luxury. I get that you're against my vision, but people can enjoy the rugged outdoors and still be pampered once they return to the resort. It's like outfitting a bunkhouse with cots versus feather beds. What you're sleeping on doesn't make it any less of a bunkhouse."

"It does when you're gutting the interior and exterior of the bunkhouse and then hanging a sign on the door that says yoga retreat."

"Nobody wants to gut Silver Bells. But even you must admit, it needs some serious updating. And I know you've put a lot of time, money and effort into the place. Your uncle told me everything you've done and what you have accomplished is great. But turning this ranch around is bigger than that. It costs much more money than you have. I want to preserve the log cabins, but they need renovations. Especially the bathrooms, along with all the bathrooms in the lodge. And we have many plans for that building. A state-of-the-art kitchen along with new energy-efficient windows throughout. The heating system needs an upgrade and the guest rooms need new furnishings. That's just the beginning. We want to bring the buildings back to life, not cover them up. I've done a solid year of market research and our capital partners have signed off on our ideas. We have the resources to create a beautiful resort experience, if you'll let us."

Emma wanted to say more, but already feared she'd said too much. She had agreed not to mention the sale again, at least not until she found another angle to work.

"Say I agree to your terms," Dylan began, giving her a glimmer of hope. "What are the chances of your acquisitions firm or another of your investors buying more properties in Saddle Ridge with the idea of capitalizing on your luxury spa resort? As it stands now, Saddle Ridge is a very affordable place to live. If your investors begin buying smaller mom-and-pop stores to set up high-end boutiques that will push our local businessmen and women out, which would eventually raise the median real estate prices, then the town becomes unaffordable for those who live here now. Austin, Charleston, Nashville are prime examples, never mind Aspen itself."

The man clearly did his homework. "I can't say that hasn't happened in the past and there's always that possibility. But with the increased home prices and business sales comes an influx of cash to those who sell."

"You're under the assumption it's about money. I know a lot of people here who would stay regardless of what they were offered. That and the fact we like our sleepy town just the way it is."

"If that's the case, then why are you so concerned?"

"Because there's an equal amount that would sell.

My uncle was one of them." Emma watched Dylan's knuckles turn white as he gripped the steering wheel tighter. "What about my horses? What are your plans for them?" He braked at a red light and faced her. "I know Jax had them written into the sale, despite my protests."

"Some would remain here, but others would most likely be sold."

"To who? Sold to other local ranches or sold for slaughter? And what would you do with the horses that remained during your six-month renovation?"

"They wouldn't be left to fend for themselves, Dylan. They would have caretakers assigned to them. Most likely people who are already working on your ranch. Or you, if that's what you want. We can write it into the contract." Emma hadn't expected a barrage of questions on the way back. "As for selling the horses, I can't imagine they would be sold for slaughter."

"Then you have a lot to learn about the horse industry." Dylan held up his hand to stop her from saying anything further as he stepped on the accelerator. "I said I wasn't going to do this and I won't debate it further. It doesn't matter what your answer is, I'm not selling."

Emma remained silent for the remainder of the short drive, chastising herself for once again blowing her opportunity to change Dylan's mind. His questions were valid and had piqued her curiosity. She hadn't thought about who the horses would be sold to before. Now she wondered herself.

By the time they reached the ranch, Emma was

barely able to keep her eyes open. She hadn't slept much last night courtesy of the butter bean. Tired as she was, the massive Christmas tree at the front entrance of the Silver Bells lodge snapped her awake.

"Oh, how pretty!" Large silver bell ornaments glistened in the morning sun on the two-story tree. "How did you get it up and decorated so fast?"

Dylan cut the engine and silently stared at her as if she had two heads.

"What? Am I not supposed to ask questions, now?"

"No, you can ask whatever you'd like."

"Then what's the problem? Don't you like Christmas?" she asked.

Dylan laughed. "I love Christmas. I'm just surprised you didn't notice that blue spruce yesterday or during your previous visits to the ranch. It's been growing in that very spot probably since before you were born. We always decorate it on the first of December."

How could she have missed a giant Christmas tree? How could she have missed the tree period since it was a permanent fixture?

Dylan hopped out of the truck and held the passenger door open for her. "Maybe you need to slow down a little and appreciate what's in front of you instead of trying to change what you never really saw in the first place." He held out his hand to help her step down onto the pavement. "Humor me for a second. Do your new plans for the ranch include this tree? Or was it eliminated from the architectural drawings?"

Emma shook her head. "I don't remember seeing

it on any of the sketches. I can only assume it was removed to showcase the lodge's facade instead of hiding it."

"Is that how you see it right now? A tree covering up a building?"

"No." Emma's palm seared against his. "It's the most beautiful Christmas tree I've ever seen. And I've seen Christmas all over the world. I get what you're saying. It does enhance the place. It doesn't detract from it. I'm ashamed to admit I hadn't noticed it before."

"Then it would be fair to say you may have overlooked other parts of the ranch as well?"

Emma released his hand. "Possibly, but you can't disregard all my suggestions because I overlooked a tree. Based on what your uncle told me, even you've admitted the ranch needs more updates than you can afford."

"You still don't get it, do you?" Dylan held open the lodge entrance door for her. "If you can miss something as big as a tree, you're running in the wrong gear. I know Saddle Ridge isn't where you had planned to spend Christmas. Since you're stuck here, take the time to get to know some of my employees. Now that the roads are open, go in to town and meet people. Go baby shopping. You can send things back to Chicago after the holiday. You're surrounded by the Swan Range and Mission Mountains. Enjoy the scenery and focus on your daughter. I'm sure your job will understand when you tell them you're laid up for medical reasons. And we have Wi-Fi so it's not like you're cut off from the outside world."

Emma closed her eyes. She already dreaded telling Charlie about her travel restrictions. Knowing him, he'd see it as another advantage. And if she returned to Chicago after two weeks without a contract in hand, she'd be lucky to still have any job at the firm.

"Thank you for yesterday, this morning and in advance for the next two weeks." She dug in her bag for her room key.

Emma didn't wait for him to respond. She was in desperate need of a shower and a change of clothes. She wound her way past the numerous poinsettia plants surrounding the front desk and then looked up and saw the enormous Christmas wreath hanging from the second-floor balcony and the garland draped along the railing on either side of it. *Could she have been that blind?* She wanted to believe Dylan was playing a colossal joke on her. As much as she wanted to think it wasn't her fault, he was right.

She had been laser focused on acquiring Silver Bells. What was wrong with that, though? So she was career-oriented. She had goals she wanted to obtain for her and her daughter. Financial security was everything. She had two weeks to come up with an alternate plan and she'd stop at nothing to succeed. Her daughter's future depended on it.

Chapter Seven

Outside of lunch, Emma spent much of the day in her room napping. Now she was wide awake and probably would be for the rest of the night. An hour ago, Dylan had phoned her room to check up on her. She wondered why he had made the call himself instead of asking the front desk to do it, then she figured after he'd seen her at her worst, the formality of their relationship had gone out the window.

To her surprise, he asked if she would be interested in going on a group sleigh ride, and even warned that if she did, she had to either ride up front with him or Wes, because the seats had already been reserved by couples. After Sandy had mentioned sleigh riding yesterday, she didn't care where she rode as long as she got to go. She had never thought she'd have the opportunity to ride in an open sleigh and refused to pass up the chance.

The crisp sting of cold Montana air against her cheeks couldn't quell her excitement. The landscape was majestic once she took the time to appreciate it. Last night's snow had heavily blanketed the trees. The below-freezing temperatures had created a thin ice-covered crust on top of the snow, creating a diamond-like sparkle. And when the winds gently blew, the horizon exploded in a magical dance of glistening elegance. She thought she had stepped into a photograph. Mother Nature had outdone herself.

Dylan and Wes approached their group wearing bright red snow pants and heavy black boots. Their red parkas hung open revealing red suspenders over white thermal shirts. Santa wished he looked that sexy. They led two teams of palomino-colored Belgian draft horses pulling two large red sleighs. Actual sleighs, like in the Christmas song! Emma practically bounced up and down like a little kid.

When Sandy had mentioned sleigh riding yesterday, she thought she was joking. Today at lunch Emma had asked what horse breeds the ranch owned. Dylan's question about who they would be sold to after the sale still bothered her and she wanted to learn all she could about the magnificent animals.

It puzzled Emma why Silver Bells wasn't advertising sleigh rides and snowcat tours. After scouring their website again, she finally found mention of both tour packages at the end of the booking page. Both items needed to be front and center. From a tourist's standpoint, those activities would have drawn her in. But there was no mention of either in their brochures, which were sparse and outdated. They didn't even mention Wi-Fi. It baffled her and explained why the new competition had gobbled up their customers. She'd love to see the ranch's marketing budget.

"Okay, momma-to-be. You get to board first." A sexy cowboy Santa jarred her back to reality. "Do you want to ride with me or my brother?" Dylan asked.

"I guess you," Emma answered wondering how he would have reacted if she had said Wes.

Dylan guided her to the first row of the sleigh. He had lined the front seat with layers of faux fur blankets to keep her warm while the rest of the rows only had a wool blanket. He had expected her to choose him and it made her feel like a princess in one of those Hallmark movies. Okay, so Dylan was no Prince Charming, and she had never seen a pregnant princess in a fairytale, but she allowed herself the fantasy for a few minutes. Work be damned, she was going to enjoy every second of her sleigh ride.

Dylan slid in beside her. The length of his strong, muscular body pressed against her side as he picked up the reins and clucked his tongue. The sound of sleigh bells jingled as the horses plodded through the snow with ease. She never imagined herself riding in a horse-drawn sleigh through the Montana wilderness. Okay, so it wasn't exactly the wild here on the ranch, but close enough to it.

"I don't think I've seen anyone smile that big before," Dylan said.

"You have no idea." Emma looked behind her to see if the other passengers were as excited as she was. Some of them came close, but she owned it. "I've wanted to do this since I was old enough to know what a horse-drawn sleigh was. It's near the top of my bucket list."

"I knew it. I knew you had a list." Dylan laughed.

"Doesn't everybody?"

Dylan shrugged. "I don't."

"Sure you do. It doesn't have to be written down to be a bucket list." Emma nudged him playfully with her elbow. "Come on, what's something you absolutely must do before you die?"

"Raise a family."

And in the frigid cold of the Montana winter, Emma melted.

EMMA'S ENTHUSIASM WAS contagious. Even he found himself in a better mood than he'd been in all day. "Why don't you lead us off in *Jingle Bells*?"

"Me?" She laughed heartily. "I don't sing. At least not very well."

"The horses don't mind and neither do I." He playfully nudged her arm. "Entertain us."

For someone who didn't sing, she didn't take much coaxing. She belted out the song at the top of her lungs and then actually looked surprised when the rest of the group joined in. Within minutes, their sleigh was out-singing his brother's.

He sighed at the realization these moments with his brother were about to end. He'd miss Wes once he moved. One more loss to add to the list. Regardless of how he felt, he couldn't fault him for wanting to move on with his life.

In a way, he was beginning to understand what Jax had meant when he told Emma one of the reason's he was selling was so Dylan could move on from Lauren and the kids. His uncle didn't realize he had made that transition years ago. A part of him wondered if Jax sensed he was going to die. Was that what drove him to sell the place Dylan always assumed he had loved more than life? If the sale had happened first, Dylan would have had money without any responsibilities. But Jax had failed to realize that the responsibility of the ranch made him happy. Now more than ever, he wanted to keep Silver Bells in memory of his uncle. Maybe listening to Emma's presentation would give him ideas on how to save the ranch.

After an hour-and-a-half long sleigh ride, Dylan and Wes dropped their guests off in front of the lodge. Sandy had warm apple cider, hot chocolate and cookies waiting for the guests while Dylan and Wes finished tending to their teams.

After they had joined everyone at the lodge, Wes disappeared within minutes. Probably with whatever single woman was available. His brother believed in loving and leaving them fast before either of them got attached. Dylan on the other hand, hadn't been with anyone since Lauren.

He set out in search of Emma, hoping the ride hadn't been too much for her. Although, by the looks of things, she'd had the time of her life. And that's what he wanted her to experience every day.

He found her sitting in the same chair by the fireplace that he had helped her out of only two days prior. This time, she was holding Melinda's infant daughter in her arms. He couldn't imagine another woman looking more beautiful or natural holding a baby than Emma Slade.

Sheridan!

Her last name was Sheridan. Dylan couldn't believe his subconscious gave her his last name. Sure, he was attracted to Emma and had even enjoyed getting to know her better over the past few days, but that's where it ended. He had too much going on in his life even to consider marriage to anyone. Especially when he had zero claim to her child.

No.

Definitely not.

Dylan shook his head. He and Emma weren't anything other than two people thrown together by happenstance. If she hadn't been after the ranch, neither one of them would have ever given the other a second look. Okay, so he would have looked. But she wouldn't have.

"Do you have a tick or something?" Luke interrupted his thoughts.

"What? No. Why?" Dylan stared at the man.

"You're shaking your head like the dogs do when something's biting at them." Luke looked from Dylan to Emma and back again.

"Oh. Now it makes sense."

"What makes sense?" Dylan felt his good mood beginning to slip away.

"Emma's caught your eye. Sandy told me there was some romance brewing between the two of you."

"Sandy needs to stop spreading rumors." Dylan rolled his eyes. "I assure you, there is nothing going on except genuine concern for her and her daughter. I thought she was losing that baby. I've never seen someone so scared in my entire life. Never mind how terrified I was. But they're safe now, and I'll make sure they continue to be safe for as long as she's here."

"Yep. You've got it bad, man." Luke slapped him on the back. "She looks pretty good holding that baby, doesn't she?"

Dylan took off his hat and whacked Luke with it. "I do not have it bad for her." Suddenly the room felt hot and for a minute, he thought he might suffocate. He had no romantic feelings for Emma whatsoever. And he planned to keep it that way.

AFTER HER HEART slowed to a normal rate, Emma began to enjoy holding Gabriella in her arms. She had always heard people say nothing smelled better than a baby. She couldn't fathom what they meant. She had always equated babies with smelly diapers and sour spit-up. Now she understood the meaning. Gabriella had a certain scent. It was like a new car scent for humans. It was innocent and clean.

And those tiny fingers! Gabriella wrapped her hand around Emma's index finger and didn't let go. She couldn't believe the amount of strength a six-month-old had. She was a bundle of perfection, making Emma even more excited to meet her own daughter. The next eight weeks would be agonizingly slow. And she still wasn't the least bit prepared.

Hopefully the doctor would clear her after the two weeks, but there weren't any guarantees. She wondered if she ordered baby items online if they would arrive at the ranch before she left for home due to the holidays. She couldn't have them sent to her apartment in Chicago because nobody was there to receive them. She could try shopping in town, not that she expected them to have anything that she needed.

She had handled her entire pregnancy poorly. She'd put everything baby-related on the back burner while she focused solely on her career. It hadn't mattered how many times she had sworn she wouldn't repeat her mother's patterns, because that was exactly what she had done.

She should have completed her daughter's nursery already. Her desk and bookcases along with boxes of client research files still filled the room. She couldn't move them until she figured out how to make an office fit elsewhere in the apartment. She needed to get rid of half of what she owned to make room for the baby's things. The office was a definite must, so either the living room or the dining area needed to go. Eating at a table was overrated, anyway.

None of it may matter, though. She'd have to move into a one-bedroom elsewhere if she didn't close this deal. The lower salary of her demoted position wouldn't cover her current rent.

Anxiety rapidly replaced Emma's short-lived baby joy.

"Are you all right?" Melinda asked.

"No. I'm not." Gabriella began to cry in her arms. Melinda lifted the baby and gently rocked her.

"It's okay. She's just picking up on your tension. You should be happy. You're about to have a baby."

"I don't know what I'm going to do."

"Talk to us." Sandy perched on the overstuffed arm of the chair. "Maybe we can help."

"I wish it were that simple." Emma filled in Melinda, Rhonda and Sandy about her apartment situation. She left out the part regarding the sale of the ranch. As far as they knew, the deal was off. They'd hate her if they found out she still intended to change Dylan's mind.

"I don't know much about Chicago, but I can tell you downsizing was the best thing I've ever done," Rhonda said. "I had an apartment before I started working here a few years ago. It was filled with more crap than I knew what to do with. I was juggling multiple jobs depending on the season. I was working non-stop to keep a roof over all my possessions. Then I realized they were possessing me. When Jax told me that room and board were part of my salary here, I hesitated to accept the job. I went home and took inventory of everything I owned. You know what? Ninety percent of it was stuff I could live without. I sold some of it, gave the rest away and moved in here. I have more money now, even though I make less cash because of the room and board. You might be surprised with what you can do without."

"I don't mean to sound harsh." Melinda continued to rock Gabriella, who had gone from crying to cooing. "But I'm a single mom living with an infant in one room that doesn't even have a kitchen in it. Is it ideal? No, but it's not impossible. Regardless whether you move or not, don't get hung up on having a separate office space or a separate baby space. Your daughter isn't going to care if she shares a room with you or if the walls are painted pink. Baby furniture can be ordered online and if you don't have anyone to put the crib together for you, buy from a local store and pay the extra charge for them to put it together or get a portable crib. I don't mean one of those fabric and mesh play yards, I mean a wooden portable crib on wheels. They fold open, set up in seconds and look like a real crib. You can wheel it right into your bedroom. If you're anything like me, you'll want your baby sleeping near you at night."

"One trip to Walmart and you'll be able to pick up all the necessities or you can order it all online and have it shipped," Sandy chimed in. "Melinda had a baby registry there."

They made it sound so logical. "I don't have a baby registry."

"Guess what we're doing after dinner?" Rhonda wrapped an arm around her shoulder. "You've got this, girl. Just remember, the simpler you keep things, the easier they are to change down the line."

A couple hours later, Emma had successfully filled out her baby registry with the womens' help. Even if no one purchased a single item, she had a list of everything she needed and could order it all with a few simple clicks.

Feeling more in control, Emma headed back to her room. She scanned the great room and dining area along the way, hoping to see Dylan. She still needed to convince him to sell, although now it felt like a betrayal to her newfound friends.

He'd kept his distance from her since they'd arrived back at the lodge. She had expected him to join her for dinner as he had during previous meals, but instead he fixed a plate and disappeared. It was as if a switch had flipped when he saw her holding Gabriella. Maybe he'd gotten a good dose of her soon-to-be reality. She couldn't fault him for it. Men didn't want to be bothered with pregnant women.

Two hours later, Dylan texted Emma to meet him in what used to be Jax's old office near the rear of the lodge and he'd listen to her proposal. She didn't even know he had her number. But it didn't matter. She finally had her chance and she refused to blow it.

He silently held the door for her as she entered. No hello, how are you? No greeting of any kind. She could understand him wanting to get down to business, but this bordered on rudeness.

"Are you ready to get started? You have an hour." All friendliness had vanished from his voice, leaving behind a cold detachment. She wondered if he'd have more warmth toward a total stranger.

"Did I upset you in some way?" Emma asked. There was no point in giving a presentation to a contentious audience. She already felt as if she was wasting both of their time.

"You've asked me for this repeatedly and I'm giving it to you. What's the problem?"

Emma sat her bag on the chair across from his

desk. "You could at least be cordial." When he didn't respond, she almost turned around and walked out. A soft kick from her daughter reminded her how much rode on this presentation. "Where can I set up?"

They both looked around the room. Stacks of papers, folders and worn loose-leaf binders littered every hard surface. The office had been disorganized when she'd met Jax there, but not to this extent.

"What happened in here?" she asked.

"I did." Dylan grabbed an empty file box from the floor and began piling papers into it. He set it on top of a haphazard stack of folders. "My uncle's so-called filing system is getting the best of me." He faced her, making eye contact for the first time since she'd walked through the door. "Question… Did Jax disclose all of the ranch's debt during your negotiations?"

"Yes. It was part of our due diligence. I can email you the spreadsheet."

Dylan laughed. "A spreadsheet. That would have been nice to have had earlier. You'd think he'd have his own."

"He did. At least, I sent him mine for his approval."

Dylan sat down behind the desk. "I still haven't figured out how to access his email. I'd appreciate seeing what you have. I'm just glad my uncle had the foresight to make me the only heir to his estate or else I'd be scrambling to find a way to buy out my brothers. Jax had every scenario covered in the event of illness or death."

"I know." Emma unzipped her laptop case. "He didn't want to leave anything to chance."

"How would you know that?" The gruffness in his voice took her by surprise. She looked up to see him staring at her incredulously.

"That's part of what we do. We examine all contractual documentation, which is why the process takes so long." She set her computer on the desk. "Your uncle couldn't have sold the ranch without your shares. Why did you go along with it if you were that set against it? You could have bought him out."

Dylan reclined in his chair and regarded her silently before answering. Charlie did the same thing when she asked a question and it bugged the heck out of her. It was as if they were weighing what they should or shouldn't say around her.

"My family has gone through a lot of heartache and misery in recent years. Fighting my uncle would have torn it apart further. Neither of us could afford to buy the other out. The ranch was our life. Silver Bells is all we own after investing every penny we had into it."

Emma hadn't realized how tight Dylan's financial situation was, which made selling even more logical to her. "What were you planning to do after the ranch sold?"

"I hadn't committed to anything yet. My share of the sale would have been decent but not nearly enough to buy another guest ranch. I was interested in a place not far from here, but they had to come way down on the price. The day I made up my mind to buy it, someone else beat me to it with a full price offer. I couldn't counter at that point. Not that it matters anymore. I can float the ranch for only so long. And from the debts I discovered tonight, I won't be able to float it for as long as I thought. I'm curious to see how much debt your spreadsheet tells me I still haven't found."

"Is that why you're willing to listen to my proposal? Because of Jax's debt?" Emma hated being Dylan's last resort. Yes, she wanted him to sell, but because he saw a future and happiness elsewhere. Not because he didn't have any other choice.

"I looked at a few smaller places—around ten to fifteen acres at most—just to live on, but that will tie up my money in case I find a guest ranch I can afford. I had just begun to expand my search into Wyoming near my brother Garrett when Jax died." The leather chair creaked as he tilted it back and rocked. "It's ironic, isn't it? I'm the sole owner of a guest ranch—which is what I wanted—but I can't afford to update it. You already knew that, though. Just like you apparently know more about the ranch finances than I do. Hell, after what you told me yesterday, you may have even known Jax better than me."

Emma didn't like the undercurrent of the conversation. "There's no need to take this out on me." If Dylan wanted to vent, she'd listen, but she wasn't going to tolerate his anger when she had done nothing wrong. "I get that you're upset, but don't get mad at me because of your uncle's lack of communication."

Dylan placed both hands on the desk and slowly rose. "You're right. I'm sorry." He picked up her laptop and handed it to her. "I think we should table this presentation for another time. I'm discovering more than I had anticipated about a lot of things."

Emma jammed the computer into the case and slung the strap over her shoulder. "That's fine." She turned and reached for the door, leaving him to wallow in his misery.

"Nah, honey, I mean it. I really am sorry."

Emma sighed. She should keep going and not look back. After all, tomorrow was another day. Nope… Even channeling her inner Scarlett O'Hara wouldn't save her from his ornery Rhett Butler attitude.

She turned to face him. "We don't have to discuss work. If you want a shoulder to lean on, I'm available. We're stuck here together. Might as well make the best of it, right? I thought we were becoming friends."

"I don't want to be friends with you."

"Wow! You don't mince words, do you?"

"Nope."

"Well, I'm certainly not staying where I'm not wanted." He'd passed rudeness and gone straight to impertinent ass. Emma stormed out of his office and through the lodge, hoping nobody would see her. She'd been a fool to allow any man to get under her skin during her pregnancy. Romance wasn't an option. There wasn't room in her heart for anyone except her daughter, and she had already neglected her daughter's needs because of some tired old ranch. She'd jeopardized her and her baby's health in order to convince Dylan Slade to change his mind. No job was worth that risk.

Charlie had offered to send someone in her place

twice and she had said no. If she had agreed and they succeeded in finalizing the paperwork, she still would have had a 50-50 chance of getting her promotion, since the majority of the work had been hers and they couldn't penalize her for being pregnant. Instead, she had balked at the idea of allowing anyone to help her because she didn't like their condescending attitude. She had learned a long time ago that in business there were times when swallowing your pride was necessary. This was one of them.

She jammed the key into the lock of her door. Tomorrow she would look into finding a new place to stay. Even if Dylan had listened to her presentation, it wouldn't have mattered. He'd made up his mind and she had made up hers. It was time to give up.

"You don't understand." Suddenly, Dylan was behind her and filled her doorway before she had a chance to shut the door.

Emma tossed her laptop case on the bed and faced him. "I understood you perfectly."

Dylan closed the distance between them in two long strides. "Being friends with you means not being able to touch you. Not being able to kiss you or hold you in my arms." He held her face in his hands. "Dammit woman, I lose my senses when I'm around you."

His mouth crashed down upon hers, claiming every bit of resolve she had left. She wanted to push him away and avoid the roller coaster of emotions that were certain to accompany this—whatever this was.

Instead, she pulled him closer, tasted him deeper and allowed him to brand her with his kisses.

They broke apart and in between panted breaths he whispered, "I don't know you well enough to ask you to stay, but I know enough not to let you go. Not yet."

"This is crazy." Her hands splayed across his chest, wanting to push him away…knowing nothing good could come out of this. His fingers lightly trailed down her neck and shoulders until his arms wound around her, drawing her closer to him. "This can never work. *We* can never work."

Dylan eased her toward the bed. "I know we can't. That doesn't mean we can't enjoy the next two weeks together." He shifted her body, so he could sit on the edge of the bed while she stood in front of him. He lifted her hands and placed them on her belly. Covering them with his own, he smiled as he looked up at her. "Let's see where this takes us. Maybe it won't lead to anything more than a beautiful Christmas memory. Then again, maybe it will be the first of many Christmas memories."

Dylan said the words any woman would love to hear. Any woman who wasn't pregnant and didn't live sixteen hundred miles away. "Dylan, be realistic. I live in Chicago and I come with an eighteen-year commitment. A child is a surreal thought, even for me, and I'm the one who's pregnant. I can't imagine anyone wanting to take on that responsibility."

"It's not an unfamiliar responsibility to me. I've been a father before. And I would've continued being one if my marriage hadn't fallen apart. My father was a family man and he raised me to be the same way. Children don't scare me. But the thought of not having the chance to find out if there is more between us terrifies me. I realized that today."

"Is that why you disappeared after you saw me holding Gabriella?"

"Yes and no. That only confirmed it. It began to hit me this morning when I was driving to the hospital. I realized I couldn't wait to see you. And when the doctor said you had to stay in town for two weeks, I panicked. You were too close and I knew I'd be too tempted to see if we had a chance. And I was right. Between the sleigh ride and seeing you with a baby, I knew I had to find a way out. So I dove into my uncle's finances, hoping I could find a missing bank account or some way to make you leave and stay away for good. Then it hit me. I didn't want you to go."

"But I can't stay, either." Emma crossed the room to gain whatever space she could from him. She needed to think clearly and rationally and being near him clouded her judgment. "All we have are these two weeks, and then I'm gone. I won't change my mind, Dylan, just as you won't change your mind and sell me the ranch. Why did you ask me to give you my presentation tonight?"

"Because I wanted to steal your ideas and see if I could use them to find my own investors."

"Wow." Her heart sank into the pit of her stomach. "That's honest."

Dylan rose from the bed. "I'd never be anything but honest with you."

"But you're not being honest with yourself. So I'll have to be honest enough for the both of us." Emma willed herself to deny him. "I don't think I'm strong enough for a two-week fling with you. Not because I'm afraid I'll stay. I know I won't. I'm afraid my heart will shatter when I leave."

"Then let me hold it in the palm of my hand and keep it safe. Give us a chance."

Emma closed her eyes. Her heart told her to say yes while her brain screamed no!

No!

No!

"Yes, let's make a Christmas memory."

Chapter Eight

The following morning Dylan stumbled into the kitchen and started a pot of coffee in the old stainless steel percolator. Modern had been a foreign concept to Jax. Even his old beat-up Jeep Wagoneer was over fifty years old. The thing ran beautifully though, so Dylan couldn't fault the man too much.

Jax had taken good care of everything he owned and Dylan wouldn't change much of the log home's rustic charm. The kitchen appliances could use some updating and the butcher-block countertop needed sanding and resealing. The custom handmade cabinets could stand refinishing, as could the floors. All things Dylan could easily handle. He'd change out some of the dated furniture, but the bones of the structure weren't that bad. At almost three thousand square feet, the house would be a great place to raise a family.

The sun wasn't even up and he already had a headache. He pulled out a chair and sat at the kitchen table, which had notes strewn across it. He hadn't meant to spend half the night in Emma's room, but after she had agreed to give them a chance, she offered to show him the ranch presentation. He didn't ask why, since he'd already admitted to wanting to use her ideas. He didn't know if it was her last ditch effort to change his mind and be able to honestly tell her boss she'd given it her all, or if she was trying to help him. Either way, he had listened to every word she said. While the majority of it went against the cowboy way of life, she had some solid ideas that he would have loved to work in to the ranch.

The state-of-the-art kitchen would allow the ranch to book weddings and other events. They handled some weddings here and there, but an outside vendor had catered most of them. Providing in-house catering along with an event planner would allow them to offer destination wedding packages.

He tried to hide his embarrassment when Emma pulled up their website. He knew it was outdated and he had talked to Jax a few times about having it redesigned. But after astronomical quotes, Jax had nixed the idea. It was on his current to-do list, but the ranch didn't have the extra thousands of dollars to spare. When Emma told him there were ways to have sites designed for free by college students trying to make a name for themselves, he realized he had options. She even took the time to show him other guest ranches and pointed out key features that drove business to their sites. By the time she was through, he understood why the business was struggling.

Dylan wasn't up on the latest technology. He'd spent most of his life outdoors, working with his hands and animals. Some of her ideas along with the keyless entry system she had mentioned were well out of his realm of expertise. He still couldn't figure out what the problem was with using a regular key. A lot less went wrong when you kept it simple.

When he left her room sometime after midnight, he hadn't told her his plans one way or the other. He knew she was disappointed with his silence, but at the time, he hadn't completely made up his mind. The more he thought about last night and the more notes he took, the more of a future he saw for Silver Bells. As a guest ranch, not a luxury spa.

His decision killed any chance Emma had at getting her promotion. That was a guilt he wasn't ready to face. He didn't want to string her along, either. Unless he could convince her to stay in Montana. But he wanted the decision to be her choice. He'd love to hire her as the lodge's manager, knowing the place would have a fighting chance with her on board. It had been a job both Dylan and Jax had shared and it needed one person's entire attention. He'd still need to find an investor or two, but that seemed more obtainable if she signed on.

Dylan poured a cup of coffee, laughing at the irony of the situation. Emma had come to Saddle Ridge to change his mind, now he had to find a way to change hers. That meant he had to remain on his best behavior and not only convince her to stay past New Year's Day, but to give their relationship the courtesy of acknowledging it could be more than a two-week fling. Dating Emma and her accepting the position didn't necessarily have to go hand-in-hand. But after she had agreed to give them a chance while she remained in town over the holidays, hope began to grow inside him. Not just for them as a couple, but for the ranch, as well. He had his work cut out for him. He wanted her to live in the very place she wanted to change.

A hard knock followed by his back door opening snapped him back to the present. Wes strode in still wearing yesterday's clothes. His brother grunted hello as he poured a cup of coffee and then flopped into a kitchen chair.

"Rough night?"

"Yeah." Wes flipped through Dylan's notes. "Still at it huh?"

Dylan joined him at the table. "I have some new ideas. I just need someone willing to invest in the ranch."

"So nothing I said yesterday convinced you to change your mind?" Wes asked.

"I can't walk away."

"Well, good luck, then." Wes sipped his coffee.

"Don't sound too enthusiastic." Dylan gathered up his paperwork and stacked it in the center of the table before his brother saw the sketches of the rocking horse.

"No, I mean it. I hope you do save Silver Bells. Just because I don't want to stay in Saddle Ridge doesn't mean I don't want you to be happy here. Speaking of happy, what's going on with you and the pregnant woman? Isn't she public enemy number one?"

"Not so much anymore. We have agreed to see where the next two weeks take us."

"You can't be serious?" Wes rocked his chair back onto two legs. "Man, you don't learn from your mistakes, do you?"

"What's that supposed to mean?"

"How is the situation any different from you and Lauren? Once again, you want a city girl with children to move on the ranch with you. How did that work out for you the first time?"

"Lauren wasn't a city girl and Emma has one kid. At least she will soon." Emma's situation was completely different from Lauren's, but he didn't feel the need to justify it to Wes.

"The fact Lauren wasn't a city girl should be even more of a red flag. Emma is way more city than Lauren and look how that turned out. Why do you want to put yourself through this again? These women don't want to live way out on an isolated ranch. Look what happened to Harlan and his first wife. Same thing."

"Molly had other issues going on, too. This place isn't isolated. We have people coming and going year round."

"Yep. Other people are coming and going from this place and you and Jax and everyone else who worked here never got off the ranch. You're proving my point. You're looking for any excuse to convince yourself that this will work." Wes rocked forward until all four chair legs were on the floor. "Hey, for your sake, I hope I'm wrong. Maybe she's a country girl at heart who likes the outdoors but just hasn't found a way to cut ties with Chicago. Either way, good luck. I need to head home and shower."

"Don't let me stop you." Dylan mentally tabulated the chances Wes was right about Emma. Was he making the same mistake?

"By the way, the reason I stopped in here this morning wasn't to harass you. Billy Johnson got into a bad snowmobile wreck. He might lose his leg. I spent most of the night in the hospital with his wife. I tried to call but couldn't reach you. Just thought you'd want to know since he used to work here. His family is going to need some extra support and I thought it would be nice if we took up a collection for him with it being Christmas. They are going to have it pretty rough. His new health insurance hasn't kicked in yet and he couldn't afford to continue paying on the old insurance without the ranch's percentage."

"Oh, man." Dylan's phone had died when he was with Emma. He'd put it on the charger last night but had forgotten to turn it back on. Billy had been their ranch manager. The man was in his midforties with a wife and four kids. He had hated losing him as an employee but understood his reasons for taking another offer and not wanting to wait and see if Dylan could save the ranch. They had talked at length and Dylan told him there would always be a place for him if he wanted to return. "I'll let everyone know about Billy. This is just another reason why I need to keep this place going."

"How would that have saved Billy?" Wes set his mug in the sink. "The accident wasn't related to his job."

"No, but he would have still had insurance. Those medical bills may wipe them out."

"Yeah, you're right. That does make a difference." Wes headed for the door. "Thanks for the coffee. I'll see you in a bit."

Dylan spread the notes across the table, more fired up than he had been fifteen minutes ago. He needed to create his own presentation to give to potential investors. It wouldn't be fancy or animated like Emma's had been, but he knew how to work a computer. In the end, only the facts mattered. He couldn't lose another employee or allow another person to go without health insurance. He refused to let anyone else suffer because of his and Jax's mismanagement. He had to right the wrong, and as guilty as he may feel for borrowing Emma's ideas, he had to push that aside. Too many families depended on him. Emma would understand. She had to.

EMMA HAD NEVER been happier to see a washing machine and dryer in her entire life. The ranch had an on-site mini laundromat and she had managed to wash a small load of whites and darks before breakfast. She planned to head into town later and check out the local shop situation. She didn't have high hopes for it, but it would be a new adventure just the same. Hopefully she could find some things to last her the next two weeks.

Emma tried to avoid maternity clothes. She couldn't see spending money on something she would only wear for a few months. She made a decent salary but it didn't allow her to spend her earnings foolishly. She had to watch every penny with the butter bean on the way. Granted, there were some things like underwear and pants that couldn't be avoided, but for the most part she had managed to wear loose fitting tops that she could get away with after she gave birth.

Her friend, Jennie, told her she'd probably get sick of those clothes by then. And she may be right. Her fisherman's knit sweater had lost its appeal a month ago. She needed to buy a pair or two of shoes in a bigger size. She felt larger than life over the past few days and she still had a little over seven and a half weeks to go.

The lodge employees were in a somber mood when she entered the dining area. The little talking she heard was hushed. She spotted Dylan and wondered if he had told them about her presentation last night. She scanned their faces. Could she live with uprooting so many people's lives?

"Good morning," Dylan greeted her.

"Is it?" Emma looked around. "What's going on?"

"I just finished telling them that a former employee got into a terrible accident last night. He may lose his leg. Four kids, a wife and no insurance."

"Oh, that's awful." Emma sensed some blame behind his words. "Did he leave recently?"

Dylan nodded. "Shortly after Jax told him we were selling the ranch. The accident had nothing to do with that. Not having insurance sure did, though."

"I'm sorry he and his family are suffering." Emma wondered if any of her new friends blamed her the way Dylan did. "Please let me know if there's anything I can do."

"We're taking up a collection to help pay their bills. We've decided to adopt the family for Christmas. We will head into town later and go grocery shopping for them, buy gifts for the kids, decorate and do everything we can to make their life as normal as possible during this time. It would be great if you joined us."

Emma nodded, unable to speak. Helping the family was the very least she could do. She would talk to Charlie later and see if the firm would donate to the family. She had closed dozens of similar deals and had never witnessed the fallout on such a personal level. Whether it was an apartment building they were turning into condominiums or a strip mall they were turning into a mega center, her firm negatively affected many lives while making their investors richer. She'd always known that and had been a willing participant. But this time she was witnessing it firsthand, and it really hit home. Now that she was getting to know many of the people here better, turning the ranch into a luxury resort spa didn't seem that wonderful, anymore. Of course, that had been Dylan's plan when he had asked her to spend time with his employees. She'd been played to a certain extent, but she was okay with it. It had opened her eyes. Emma had been eager to get off the ranch so she could gain the advantage and push Dylan to sell. Now, not so much.

"About last night…" Dylan began.

"Is this personal or business?"

"Business first."

Emma shook her head. "I don't want to talk business right now. It hardly seems appropriate and I don't want anyone to know what we have discussed. I know what your answer is going to be, and that's fine."

"Well, that's not quite what I wanted to talk about, but it can wait."

They stood staring at each other halfway between the tables and the empty buffet line. When Dylan didn't continue to the personal side of the conversation, she shrugged and made her way to the French toast. Which reminded her of France and the baby name book she had downloaded.

She had always been partial to French names for some reason. She'd only been to Paris once, but had visited the French countryside many times on business. Her favorite place had been the small picturesque town of Vienne along the Rhone River. Vienne Sheridan had a nice ring to it. But she wondered if too many people would mistake it for Vienna or Vivian?

Emma checked to see if Dylan had followed her to the line. He was on the phone, walking toward the front of the lodge. Maybe he had already eaten. She fixed her plate and sat quietly at a table by herself. A few of the other employees remained clustered by the fireplace, but most had already scattered. She ate in uncomfortable silence and then made her way back to her room.

Her job demanded that she follow through with everything she came to Saddle Ridge for. Work should come first, but the weather had warmed a few degrees and Emma wanted to take full advantage of what the ranch had to offer—what she could do in her condition, anyway. *So why don't you?* The doctor had told her to get light exercise and Dylan had told her to get out and meet people. After being confined to a hospital room for eighteen hours, the last thing she wanted to do was stay cooped up in her room. Emma added a few more layers to her outfit and headed out the door. Work could wait. At least a few more hours.

Snowshoeing was at the top of her list.

After borrowing a pair of boots from Sandy, another employee fitted her in a pair of wide deck shoes and helped her snap her feet into the bindings. She slipped on her jacket and gloves, made sure she had her phone and headed outside.

The slight mountain breeze didn't help cool her body, still trembling from Dylan's kiss last night. She hadn't known she could be kissed like that. She could only imagine what making love to him would feel like. No. That's the last thing she needed to do. Making love to Dylan Slade was off-limits, not to mention unprofessional. Not that kissing was professional, either.

Emma started to laugh. She didn't know which was funnier, the idea Dylan would want to make love to her while she was pregnant or the actual act itself. At this stage, she didn't think she was capable of sex, although she had heard some wild stories.

She gripped her poles as she trudged through the snow, willing sex from her brain. Despite her girth, she sank only a couple inches with each step. By the time the stables were in sight, she had worked up a slight sweat. She saw Dylan and another man heading into the second building. She stopped along one of the pasture fences and looked out over the hearty draft horse herd. They seemed to be enjoying the snow. She never knew horses could withstand such cold temperatures.

She made her way toward the second stables when she heard a man's voice.

"I know it's not what that commercial real estate firm offered you, but I can guarantee everyone immediate employment. My only condition is I need you to run the place. I've known you and Jax for a long time and I can't see the employees staying if you're not here."

"You've given me a lot to chew on." She heard Dylan say. "Are you sure you won't consider partnering with me instead of a full buyout?"

"I'm afraid not. I'd like to join the two ranches since they're next to one another. You have a lot of acreage now, but almost doubling the size would allow us to add to the amenities."

"I'm glad you reached out to me. I haven't decided anything yet, but I'll definitely let you know one way or the other."

"I look forward to hearing from you."

Emma attempted to turn around make a casual retreat, until she saw her massive snowshoe tracks in the snow. There was no hiding her presence. When the men didn't come out of the stables, she continued to the entrance and poked her head in. The building was empty.

"What are you doing out here?" Dylan said from behind her.

"Oh, hi." How did he do that? Emma attempted to remain calm. "I'm just getting my exercise."

"Are you sure snowshoeing is safe during your pregnancy?" he asked as they both watched a snowmobile drive out from behind the stables. Emma scrutinized his expression. So far, nothing screamed, *You were eavesdropping on my conversation*. Maybe she'd gotten away with it.

"Snowshoeing is a very safe sport for pregnant women. But rest assured, before I came out here, I double-checked the list the doctor gave me. Plus, I used to go snowshoeing all the time when I was in boarding school."

Dylan shook his head.

"What?" Emma asked.

"The whole boarding school thing. I don't understand why people have children if they plan on sending them away for most of their adolescent life."

She had asked herself that very same question when she was growing up. Yet she still felt the need to defend her parents' decision. "I had a great education. I learned to socialize and communicate with others well since I didn't have my parents to fall back on. Living away from home at an early age teaches you how to be strong. That being said, I have no intention of sending my daughter to boarding school, much to my parents' dismay. I want to be there for her every day she comes home from school. I want to help her with her homework, bake brownies for bake sales, go to her school recitals and be a member of that Parent-Teacher Association thing. I want my daughter to have a normal, healthy life. She'll be different from some of the kids because I'm a single mom, but I'm sure she won't be the only kid without two parents."

Dylan dug his boot into the hard-packed snow by the stables entrance. "Have you given last night's discussion any more thought?"

"The you-and-I part?" Emma tugged on his jacket, urging him to step closer. "Some. I don't know how much we can think about it without overthinking it. I wouldn't mind spending some time alone with you again, though."

"I'd like that, too." Dylan held her face in his gloved hands and kissed her softly. "How would you like to have dinner alone with me tonight at my uncle's house?" He released her face and slid his hands down her shoulders. "Before you say yes, I feel obligated to tell you I have an ulterior motive."

"You do, huh?" Emma wondered if he planned to mention the offer she had overheard.

"My uncle was a huge Christmas fan and he hadn't decorated his house before he died. I'd really like to cut down a tree and decorate it in his memory. But I don't want to do it alone. So if you'd be willing to give me a shoulder to lean on tonight, I'd appreciate it."

Tough-as-nails Dylan Slade had an even bigger

heart than she'd imagined. "I'd be honored to lend you my shoulder."

"Great, I promise to make it fun. He would've wanted it that way." Dylan gave her a quick kiss on the lips before stepping away from her. "But I have a lot to get done before then. Can you meet me at the lodge entrance at six?"

"Most definitely. I should get back to my workout." Emma wanted to stay and ask him who the man on the snowmobile had been, but she thought better of it. She gripped her poles and plodded back to the lodge. She needed to call Charlie and tell him Dylan had another offer. A small part of her was relieved it was over, because there was no way he would accept her deal over the other one, if he sold at all. The new offer guaranteed employment. A bigger part of her was devastated she would lose her promotion. That meant even more changes to her life. Starting with moving into a smaller apartment. She'd call Charlie when she got back to the ranch. Maybe they could counter with something better. Dylan's kiss was good, but she wasn't ready to give up her dream just yet.

A few hours later, Emma had a new offer from Charlie and he expected her to present it tonight. She suggested looking into the neighboring ranch as a possible expansion project or a suitable replacement if Dylan continued to stand his ground. But she refused to discuss any of it with him tonight. Dylan wanted to honor his uncle's memory and that didn't leave any room for business. She would tell him about Charlie's pending donation to Billy's family so she could get their information. But the rest could wait until the following morning. Nobody would be any wiser. She may be an aggressive businesswoman but even she had her limits.

She wanted to be there for Dylan the way he had been there for her when she was in the hospital. It would be their first official Christmas memory. And maybe it would be the only one they would share, but it would be theirs.

Chapter Nine

Dylan had just finished putting the chicken in the oven when it was time to pick up Emma from the lodge. A few of the Silver Bells' housekeeping staff had given the house a good cleaning from top to bottom earlier that day. His nerves were beginning to catch up to him as he gave everything one last perusal before heading out the door.

He pulled up to the lodge's entrance, driving Jax's red Wagoneer. It was the only vehicle he had that Emma wouldn't have to climb up in. Plus, for a car from 1967, it was a sweet ride. He especially loved the bench seats. They were perfect for getting a little closer to your date. Not that they had time to snuggle during the five-minute drive. But this did constitute a date. The first since Lauren. He was ready. And from the looks of her, so was Emma.

Dylan left the truck running as he hopped out and opened the door for her. "You look beautiful." He gave her a kiss on the cheek. "You didn't have to wait out here. I would have come in and gotten you."

"I wasn't outside for long." She eased onto the

passenger seat. "I recognized Jax's truck from my visits and I wanted to avoid any more questions. It seems everyone on the ranch knows we are having dinner together."

Dylan closed her door and ran around to slide in beside her. "Sorry. I hadn't thought about that when I asked some of the employees to help me freshen up Jax's house."

"You didn't have to go through so much trouble for me."

He found it next to impossible to focus on his driving. Thank God it was a short trip because all he wanted to do was admire her. She looked different tonight. Not just more put together, but more serene. Her hair fell in soft brown waves around her shoulders. It took every ounce of strength not to run his fingers through them to find out if they felt as soft as they looked.

"Believe me, you wouldn't want to have seen my uncle's house before we tackled it."

"I love this truck." Emma glanced around the sparse red and charcoal interior. "Especially since I didn't need a stepladder to get into it."

He detected a hint of nervousness in her laughter. "It was Jax's pride and joy." He parked in front of the log home's expansive porch and helped her out. "I just thought of something. You've probably already seen the house."

Emma shook her head. "No, actually I haven't. I always met with your uncle at the lodge. We had figured all dwellings into our proposal, but since the house wasn't part of the guest quarters, I didn't feel it was necessary to traipse through it. We planned to use it as an on-site living quarters for our firm while the project was underway and then evaluate its use during that time."

Dylan held the door open for her as she entered. "I've always loved this house. The craftsmanship is impeccable for a place that's been around for almost a hundred years. It was the first structure on the property."

Emma's mouth gaped open at the two-story interior. "This isn't what I expected at all." She ran her hands over the smooth golden logs. "I thought it would be much darker inside. This is a surprise. A very pleasant surprise."

"The chinking needs some TLC here and there, but other than that it's move-in ready." Dylan helped her out of her coat. "I know I said this already, but you look beautiful tonight."

Emma beamed up at him. "I found this great store in town today and I treated myself to something new." She ran her hands over the feminine, pale-blue sweater. "I severely under packed, not anticipating the length of my stay. I actually found quite a few places in town that I liked. I was pleasantly surprised." She wandered toward the kitchen. "What smells so amazing?"

"Chicken parmesan." Dylan strode into the kitchen and turned on the burner for the pot of water he had waiting. "With a side of pasta. I hope that's okay. I forgot to ask you what you like to eat, but I've seen you eat chicken so I took the chance."

"It's perfect. I had no idea you could cook."

"I can't make anything too elaborate, but I do all right. Between my mom and hanging around with some of the chefs here, I've picked up a few things."

Cooking for Emma suddenly became more intimate. Convincing her to stay in Montana had been his main goal, but with each passing hour, he wanted it more than he had realized.

"This is a massive kitchen. I didn't expect it to be so large for a place this old."

Emma stood at the sink and peered through the window. She looked more natural in the home than he had envisioned. His heart began to beat rapidly at the thought of raising a family with her on the ranch. Now that he had a definite way to stay on the land, he wanted to make plans for the future.

Dylan was glad he hadn't mentioned the lodge manager job to Emma earlier. Not that she had given him much of a chance. Barnaby's offer had been unexpected but not all that surprising. By combining the acreage of both ranches, they could offer more trail options and possibly even open a small downhill ski run since Barnaby's land extended into the mountains. It sounded great, but he hadn't decided to take him up on his offer yet. He still would rather maintain some ownership, but Barnaby wanted to buy the ranch outright. It was a solid plan to fall back on if he couldn't find a partner. He needed to be sure though, before he told his employees they didn't have to leave.

During the past few days, his vision had changed from saving the ranch to running the ranch with Emma by his side. The thought alone was crazy. But despite the absurdity, it felt damn right.

"It's been updated a time or two in its life. I'd like to refinish the wood surfaces throughout the house and bring out the character of the grain."

"You can do all of that yourself?"

"Sure. Woodworking is a hobby of mine, plus my father was really handy and I learned how to build just about anything from him. This house would be a great place for a bunch of kids to run around in. We loved it as children, but Jax never married or had any of his own. Would you like something to drink?"

"Just water is fine." Emma sat at the kitchen table. "I can see kids here. It has what, three bedrooms?"

"Four. But my uncle used the smallest for a study." Dylan twisted open a bottle of water and poured it into a glass for Emma. "This place has always been a second home to me, but I never fully appreciated its craftsmanship until after he was gone. It seems strange without him here."

"I bet it does. I'm glad you have the memories to look back on."

"Cheers to the memories yet to come." Dylan held up his glass to hers. "I hope you like what I have planned for after dinner."

"I thought we were decorating the Christmas tree."

"We have to get it first." Tonight's anticipation built up in him like a kid on Christmas morning. He almost wanted to skip dinner and show Emma the surprise he had planned.

"Yeah, you mentioned something about cutting one down. Wouldn't it be easier to go into town and buy one? I saw Christmas trees for sale in front of the supermarket."

"Darlin', no self-respecting cowboy buys a Christmas tree. Trust me, you'll enjoy the experience."

WHEN DYLAN UNCOVERED her eyes, she never in a million years expected to see a small white and silver sleigh harnessed to a lone Belgian.

"I feel like I've stepped into a storybook." Emma giggled as Dylan wrapped her in wool and faux fur blankets. "I can't believe this is how we're getting a Christmas tree."

"Aren't you glad we didn't go into town?"

"Absolutely!" None of her friends would ever believe she rode on a one-horse open sleigh, let alone one driven by a sexy cowboy after he'd cooked her the most incredible dinner she'd ever eaten. And that wasn't her pregnancy hormones talking, either. The man could seriously cook. The majority of her meals came from the freezer and involved her heating them in the microwave.

The pale light of the moon lit their path as their sleigh glided across the snow. Emma didn't think the smile would ever fade from her face after tonight. This moment was too perfect for words.

"I can't believe this is your life."

"What do you mean?" Dylan asked. He shifted

slightly, causing more of his body to press against hers. Emma wanted to rest her head on his shoulders, but feared she'd miss something along the way if she did.

"You live in a winter wonderland. It's like *Doctor Zhivago* meets *Frozen*."

"As beautiful as the snow is, winter can also be harsh and cruel in these parts. You have to stay prepared all season and it is a long season."

"It's not like Chicago, though. We have dirty snow."

Dylan laughed. "Give it a few days and you'll see dirty snow here, too. Of course, fresh powder will probably fall on top of it within a day or two, but it does get dirty every now and then."

They stopped at the same spot they had the other night, only tonight they could see the town with its moonlit mountains magically rising behind it.

"This would be the perfect location for an outdoor wedding chapel. Can't you just picture it right here? With a few modifications to some of the more private cabins, this could be the quintessential wedding destination in all of Saddle Ridge. It would draw people in year round with that backdrop."

Dylan could picture it very easily with Emma by his side. "I don't remember an outdoor chapel in your proposal."

"It hadn't occurred to me until now. I was remembering the first time I came to Silver Bells to meet Jax. This was the first place he showed me. Of course, in my mind I saw dollars signs and ways to capitalize on the view. I had considered another lodge of sorts right here, taking advantage of the landscape, but no matter what I came up with, they all ruined the beauty of what drew me here in the first place. That's why there aren't any new structures in my proposal. After sitting here now and the other night, I see much more. This is God's country and what better way to celebrate that than with love and marriage. I totally get why you're so protective of this place."

Dylan wrapped his arm around her and tilted her chin toward him. "I think that's the best idea you've had yet."

His lips brushed hers, gently at first before becoming more demanding. She returned his hunger as desire coursed through her veins like venom seeking a beating heart. The fervent need to make love to a man she had just gotten to know a few days prior lustfully beckoned while mocking her sensibilities. Powerless against the seduction, yet more impatient with each breath she took, for the first time in her life, Emma wanted to completely surrender to another person…to Dylan.

"Emma," he gasped. "What are you doing to me?"

"Are you asking me to stop?" She ran her tongue over his bottom lip, daring him to take her higher than she'd ever been.

"Absolutely not. I just need to know if this is leading where I think it is."

"I don't want to stop or let go of this moment. It may be all we ever have. It may be more. Whatever it is, I want to share it with you…right here under the stars in the place you love more than life itself."

Emma knew her heart would never be the same after tonight. But she was recklessly willing to take a chance on the man she suddenly didn't want to live without. She longed to be a part of his hope for the future. To share in those dreams and help him realize them without limitations. Heaven help her, she wanted Dylan Slade, in every way.

MAKING LOVE TO Emma under the Montana night sky hadn't been on his evening itinerary. Unable to resist the woman who intrigued him more than any other had, he willingly gave her the piece of his heart he hadn't believed still existed. Each kiss had driven them deeper into complete abandon. And when they had finally broken apart, his desire for her grew stronger.

Swathed in layers of warmth, he began to believe the odds were turning in their favor. Between some of Emma's proposal ideas and the wedding chapel, a clearer vision for the ranch developed in his mind. But it wouldn't be complete without Emma. He wanted to finalize the plans before asking her to stay in Montana again. He needed to offer her more than just talk and concepts. Emma required stability for her and her daughter. He couldn't ask anything of her without it.

"I promised you a Christmas tree." Dylan kissed the top of Emma's head, relishing the feel of her body against his beneath the blankets.

"No, you said we'd cut down a tree. You promised tonight would be fun." Her voice was laced with seduction, commanding his body to attention. "You definitely kept your word." Emma straddled his lap, and for the second time that evening, he lost himself within her.

By the time they arrived back at the house with their tree in tow, Dylan could barely stand. Between the day's earlier tension and the sex, all he wanted to do was crawl in bed and sleep.

"I have to tend to the horse and sleigh." Dylan kissed her in the doorway. "Will you stay the night?"

Emma nodded, her eyes heavy with sleep.

"The bedroom is at the end of the hall. It's the only one on this floor." He wanted to lift her in his arms and carry her to bed, but he knew he'd never make it outside if he did. "I'll be back shortly."

She disappeared inside as he carried the tree onto the porch. Decorating could wait another day. Tonight, he wanted to hold Emma in his arms and forget the world around them.

After unhooking the sleigh and settling his horse down for the night, he climbed in beside her sleeping form. A soft breath escaped her lips with each exhale. Not quite a snore but more of a wildcat purr. Not that he'd had the opportunity to lie down next to a wildcat. It was just the sound he imagined them having. And she had been a wildcat tonight. His wildcat.

He brushed the hair from her face and kissed her cheek goodnight. Yeah, he could definitely get used to sharing his life with Emma.

EMMA AWOKE ALONE. *Had last night been a dream?* She looked around. No, she definitely wasn't in her room at the lodge. The faint sound of whisking came from the kitchen. Emma tossed on the sweatshirt she found on a chair next to the bed and padded down the hallway.

"Good morning, sleepyhead."

"Morning." She wrapped her arms around Dylan and snuggled against his chest. "What time is it, anyway?"

"Almost nine."

"Nine? What are you still doing here?" She looked up at him, loving the day-old scruff along his jawline. "Don't you have to work?"

"I've already been out and back. Wes is handling some things for me while I take the rest of the morning off. A little break is long overdue, considering I've been pulling my weight and his around here."

Charlie's voice nagged at her from the recesses of her mind. She didn't want to hear it. Not now when things were blissfully happy between her and Dylan. "Are you making French toast?"

"I am. I know it's your favorite." He kissed the top of her head.

Emma yawned and sat down at the table. "A woman could get easily spoiled this way."

Dylan smiled, but didn't ask her to stay as he had the other night. Not that she expected him to again. Although, it would be nice to hear. The thought had crossed her mind a few times during their evening. Moving to Montana would be ludicrous and bold, even for her. She took risks in business but rarely in her personal life. As much as she had grown to admire the ranch's beauty, she still couldn't see herself living there.

"After breakfast, I thought we'd decorate the tree. Unless you have other plans."

She did. She had a date with her credit card and a baby store she saw on her way back to the ranch yesterday. But shopping could wait a little while longer. So could telling Dylan about the new offer. "Um, sure."

He expertly flipped the toast in the pan with the flick of his wrist. "That wasn't the reaction I had expected."

"I need to tell you something. Two things actually, but I don't want it to break the mood."

Dylan shut the burner off on the stove and faced her. "You have my full attention."

The smile he'd worn seconds earlier had faded into seriousness. She inwardly groaned. "I had inquired about the horses, even though you asked me not to. The horses they didn't keep would have been sold at auction. I informed my office that was unacceptable and told them it was an absolute deal-breaker. They countered and said the horses would be excluded from the deal, allowing you to decide where they went."

"That's a significant contract change." Dylan turned the burner back on and continued cooking. "I appreciate the effort. I'm still not changing my mind, but I'm glad to hear they were open to it just the same."

"Okay, well that's the one I thought would upset you."

"I'm not upset at all. I'm disheartened that your company has a complete and blatant disregard for animals, but it doesn't surprise me. They may or may not know what goes on at horse auctions. Some choose to ignore it. I'm glad you didn't. Thank you." Dylan slid the toast on to a plate and set it before her. "What's the other thing you wanted to tell me?" He sat down across from her.

"Aren't you eating?" Emma asked.

"I already did, while you were sleeping." Dylan hopped up from the table, opened the microwave and removed a small bowl. "I almost forgot. I heated up some syrup for you."

"Thank you." Emma hated when people watched her eat, but breakfast smelled too good to resist. She took a mouthful and almost dropped her fork. "These are heaven. Is that cinnamon I'm tasting? And a hint of nutmeg?"

Dylan's smile lit the room. "Now that you know my secret ingredients, I'm going to have to find a way to keep you quiet." He winked. "There's a tablespoon of sugar in there, too and one other ingredient, but I'm not telling."

"That's not right." Emma playfully nudged him with her bare feet.

"Sure it is." Dylan caught her foot in his hands and began kneading it. There was nothing like an orgasmic foot massage while eating your favorite breakfast after a night of repeated sex on the back of a one-horse open sleigh…in the snow. Yep, she'd found heaven.

"God, that feels good." The man sure knew how to treat her like a queen. "The other thing was, I told my boss about your ex-employee who got injured. The firm would like to donate twenty-five thousand dollars to his family and I will need their contact information so we can set that up for them."

Dylan stopped massaging her foot.

"Okay, that wasn't the reaction I had expected." Emma tucked her feet under her chair. "What is it?" She already knew the answer because she'd felt the same way when Charlie told her the amount. It felt like a payoff of some sort. They wouldn't have needed to worry about medical bills if Emma and her company hadn't swooped in and tried to buy the ranch.

"I don't know how Billy's wife will react to the money." Dylan jumped up from the table again and poured a cup of coffee. "She was outspoken against Jax for a while. Billy had had to run interference between the two. He hadn't liked the situation, but he understood Jax owned the ranch and could do with it as he pleased. It was no different from other corporate buyouts. Only most of the time those people kept their jobs, or at least some did."

"I get it. I'm the enemy."

Dylan reached across the table for her. "No, you're not. You were doing your job."

Were doing? She was glad she held off on mentioning the offer until later. He might reconsider the enemy part. For now, or at least for the morning, Emma wanted to leave their responsibilities behind and get lost in a little Christmas spirit.

Chapter Ten

Dylan hadn't expected to choke up while unboxing the Christmas ornaments. He hadn't realized how many his uncle had from Dylan's childhood. The realization his mother hadn't taken any of them with her to California surprised and upset him. Then again, she'd left town the day after his father's funeral. She'd put the ranch up for sale weeks later and that was when he and his brothers realized she never planned to return to Saddle Ridge.

"Some of these look really old." Emma carefully unwrapped a wad of tissue paper, revealing a delicate pale pink glass ornament.

"That was my grandmother's. No, wait. It was my great grandmother's on my mom's side." Dylan sighed. "I remember my mom hanging them high up on the tree when we were kids, for fear one of us would knock them off."

"Five boys must have been a handful." Emma rubbed her baby belly. "I'm still trying to grasp the concept of having one child, let alone that many."

"You'll do just fine." Dylan sat on the couch and

reached out for her hand, pulling Emma onto his lap. "I have faith in you."

"I can't even choose a name. I thought I had one, but the more I say Vienne Sheridan, the more it sounds like a hotel in France."

Dylan couldn't help laughing. "It kind of does." She swatted him and attempted to squirm off his lap, but he wasn't letting her go. At least not any time soon. "You could always name her Montana."

"What would be the significance?" She reached for another wrapped ornament. "She wasn't conceived here and she won't be born here."

Dylan's heart dropped into his stomach like a bowling ball in a vacuum. Granted, they hadn't settled on anything permanent, or even discussed it further, but he'd thought she would have at least considered the possibility of moving to Montana if things progressed with their relationship. He realized they had only given it a two-week timeline, but even he had hoped it would last longer than that.

"I guess you've made up your mind."

Emma stilled. "About what?" She turned in his lap to face him. "Us?"

He nodded.

"Our two weeks have just begun. I don't think that's really fair to ask me. My home is in Chicago and so is everything I own. At some point, I have to go back. I may not have a definitive birthing plan, but my doctor and my parents are in Illinois, so yes, I intend to give birth on my home turf." Emma sat the ornament on the coffee table. "Does that bother you?"

"I don't know." Dylan eased her off him and onto the couch. "I guess it does. After last night and… I don't know. I kind of wanted to be there."

"For the birth?" Emma's brows rose. "Seriously?"

Dylan had never felt more like a fool. He had no business being anywhere near the delivery room, nor did he have any claim to her child. "It was a thought. A bad one, apparently."

She reached for his hand as tears trailed down her cheeks. "Dylan."

"Emma, what is it?" He knelt before her. "Don't cry, baby."

She struggled to regain her composure. "I never thought," she said between sniffles, "that another man would want to be there for my baby that way."

Now it was Dylan's turn to breathe a sigh of relief. "Honey, babies are the most innocent creatures on earth. Just because she was conceived with someone else doesn't mean I don't have the capacity to love her."

The realization of his words almost knocked him out cold. He reached for the coffee table behind him to steady himself. He had done the one thing he swore he'd never do again. He'd fully accepted another man's child, and he hadn't even met the butter bean yet.

"Are you okay?" Emma asked, concern etched across her face. "I think I need to get you some water." She rose from the couch.

Dylan grabbed hold of her hand before she could walk away. "I don't need water." He needed something much, much stronger. "The past twenty-four hours have caught me off-guard. Your presence in my life was a complete surprise. When I'm with you, I feel like a super hero one minute and a lovesick teenager the next. You've changed my life in ways I hadn't thought possible. You opened my heart after it had been welded shut. I've devoted so much time to this ranch, I had forgotten what living feels like."

"I don't know what to tell you beyond today." Emma remained standing. "I feel guilty in so many ways."

"Why?"

"I aggressively sought out this ranch and targeted your uncle. In the process, I disrupted your life along with everybody else's who works here. I ignored my own child's needs because of this deal. I should be working on a way to convince you to sell instead of being here decorating the Christmas tree. But the truth is, I would rather be here than any other place in the world."

"I feel the same way." Dylan stood to meet her.

"I've gone from workaholic to *I need a break* in a matter of days. And while I'm sure a lot of that had to do with my labor scare, there is a whole other side of me that's tired. I'm tired of the uncertainty and the stress. I'm tired of constantly trying to get ahead. And even though I've been trying to change your mind about the ranch over the past four days, there's been a sense of relief knowing you never will. There's also deep loss I still haven't wrapped my head around. By accepting your refusal to sell, I accept that I failed.

And that failure directly affects my child. That's a hard pill to swallow. And while I'm learning to love it here, I don't think I can honestly say I'm ready to give up walking up and down three flights of stairs to get to my apartment. Or hailing a cab to buy groceries. Or listening to my neighbor's kid learn how to play the saxophone. I love Chicago. I love the noise, but I don't miss going into my office, or any of that stress. I love more about Saddle Ridge than I thought I would. And now I have a decision to make of my own. And it's a tough one because I fell hard for a cowboy."

"Really, you fell for me?" Dylan attempted to lighten the burden she carried with a bit of levity.

"Look, I realize I'm unmarried and pregnant and we just had sex on a sleigh, but I assure you, I don't make a habit out of sleeping around. I've had three relationships in my life, this being the third. I don't take anything that has happened between us lightly, but I have to ask myself repeatedly how much of it is real and how much are my hormones running in overdrive?"

"I'm real and what I feel for you is real. I know it's fast and unexpected but, honey, we can't ignore what's in front of us."

"You're right. I'm having a baby. There's no getting around it. I'd love a father for my child, but she doesn't need one to thrive. I'd love to have a man in my life to lean on when things get tough, but I can get along just fine without one. And I'd love to have somebody to grow old with and watch the butter bean grow up and have children of her own, but I can survive on my own."

"So what… You're resolved to be alone?"

"I'm not saying that at all. I'm saying for this to work I have to want you…not need you and I'm having a hard time distinguishing the two at the moment."

"I'm not." Dylan lifted her chin to him. "I want you because I'm attracted to you and I admire your strength and determination even when the odds are against you. And I need you because you've awoken me to the possibilities of tomorrow. Possibilities that only exist with you by my side. I could have asked Harlan to decorate the tree with me. He's one of the most sentimental men I know. We could have shared a beer or two and talked about old times, but I asked you. I needed the strength only you could provide."

"You don't even know me." Emma's voice was barely a whisper.

"I know enough." Dylan bent to taste her lips. Her body trembled beneath his touch as his fingers traveled down her arms and to her palms, entwining his hands with hers. He slowly lowered to his knees, and kissed her belly. "And I want to know you, butter bean. I want to see you grow up strong like your mother. She's a force to be reckoned with. Pay attention, little one. Follow your mom's lead and you can conquer the world."

Emma placed her hands on either side of his face, urging him to stand. "You sweet man. You sweet, sweet man."

Whatever beat ferociously deep within his heart was foreign to him. He'd experienced love before and it hadn't even come close. Whatever this was, he couldn't let it go without giving it everything he had. The calendar be damned. He refused to put a timeline on their relationship. However fast or whatever time they had meant nothing. All that mattered were Emma and her baby.

BY THE TIME Dylan had dropped her off at the ranch, it was well after noon. She managed to sneak in the side door without anyone seeing her. Doing the walk-of-shame wearing yesterday's clothes is always bad. Doing the walk-of-shame when pregnant was the ultimate worst.

She fumbled with the key in the lock of her room, anxious to get it open before she had to explain her whereabouts. Once inside, she collapsed against the door. Dating took a lot out of a pregnant woman.

Emma smiled when she saw the Christmas tree on the dresser. She'd never look at one the same way again. After making love twice on the way to get a tree, followed by making love all morning under it, decking the halls now had a significantly new meaning.

She crossed the room to the bed, admiring the tiny outfits she'd purchased the day before while she was in town. They had been too precious to pack away last night. They were the first clothes she had purchased for...for... She needed a name.

Emma sat on the edge of the bed and held up a tiny

red and white onesie. Technically, it was meant for Christmas, but her due date was February 11, just in time for Valentine's Day. Her daughter had to have something red to wear for the holiday. She'd blown whatever baby clothing budget she'd set. Amazingly, she didn't care.

Watching her finances was still important, but it was time to bend the rules a little. She'd been so rigid and laser focused on every detail in her life, she'd forgotten to enjoy her pregnancy. It felt good to let go. A little too good. She could really get used to living in Montana. The people, the views, the stress-free lifestyle...the lack of a job.

Reality check.

The funny thing was, the more Dylan talked about the ranch, the more she wanted to be a part of it. She had some money saved. It had originally been her job-loss contingency plan, then it morphed into the butter bean's college fund. While it was enough to carry her for a year in Chicago, it wasn't nearly enough to partner with Dylan.

Was that even an option? Every day she saw more and more possibilities for the ranch. In the same breath, with the increased proposal from her company, Dylan could have a bigger and better ranch. A place where all his employees could still work for him. But was it enough for him...and her? Silver Bells had begun to grow on her. Imagine that. The big city girl contemplating a move to the country. Her mother would die.

AFTER A DAY of shopping, a stop by town hall to pull the plats on Silver Bells and the neighboring ranch, followed by a chocolate shake and an order of fries, Emma found her second wind to do more baby shopping. She saw a crib and dresser set she loved in a baby boutique, but it wasn't practical to buy and send back to Chicago. Even if she did wind up moving to Montana, it wouldn't be until after the baby was born. Until she had a steady income to move toward, she wasn't going anywhere.

She passed a toy store, and thought about Billy Johnson's four children who wouldn't have their father home for Christmas. Her budget could go hide under the covers because she was buying those kids some presents. By the time she pulled back into the ranch, her rental car was full. Front seat, backseat and the trunk. Granted, it wasn't a very big car, but she'd done some heavy damage to her credit card.

Sandy and Melinda helped bring her packages inside. Between the women working at the ranch and some of the female guests, they spent the rest of the afternoon sitting by the fire in the great room discussing babies, men and all the mistakes they'd made with both.

"How do you know when you've found the right man and he's worth taking a leap of faith with?" Emma asked the group of women.

"You mean, how do you know you've found the right cowboy?" Sandy then proceeded to tell everyone there was a Christmas romance brewing.

"I knew there had to be something going on when

he insisted you ride up front in the snowcat," one of the guests said. "We could've made room for you in the back. It would have been a little tight, but there was room."

"He certainly is a fine specimen of a man," another said. "If I were thirty years younger and fifty pounds lighter, I'd be all over him. Emma, I'd be your biggest competition."

Everyone laughed until the man of the hour himself appeared.

"Wow, I'm so glad my employees are so fast at their jobs they have time to sit around and chat with our guests."

Emma hadn't wanted anyone to get in trouble. She'd done enough damage to the ranch as it was. "Hey now, they're just on break. They deserve a little relaxation after putting up with you for all these years."

"Yeah, don't be such a grouch." Sandy jabbed Dylan's arm. "You have a baby on the way. You should be happy."

"Sandy! I can't believe you said that." Emma turned to Dylan, pulling him into a quiet corner. "I swear I had nothing to do with that."

Dylan shrugged. "No worries. I've known Sandy since she was born. She likes to tease. That's how she landed Luke." The women's laughter reverberated behind them. "I see you did some shopping. Is this all for the baby?" He picked up a train set. "Don't you think you're getting a little ahead of yourself?"

"The pink and blue bags are for the butter bean. The rest are for the Johnson kids."

"Emma, that's a lot of stuff. You didn't have to do that."

"Yes, I did. And let's just leave it at that." Emma didn't want to rehash her guilt. She had enough of it to last a lifetime.

"How would you like to join me for dinner at Harlan and Belle's house tonight? You already know my brother, but I would like you to meet my sister-in-law. My brother Garrett and his two kids are coming in Christmas Eve. I thought it would be nice to spend some time with Belle and Harlan away from the ranch. Besides, I am sure you and Belle can spend hours talking baby."

"Taking me to your brother's house for dinner almost sounds official." Emma playfully winked at him.

"You're right, it does."

She laughed at his comment, only Dylan wasn't laughing with her. He looked painfully serious. Oh. My. God. He was making them official. Was she ready for that?

Chapter Eleven

Dylan hadn't been the least bit nervous about introducing Emma to his brother and sister-in-law until they turned off on to their ranch road. He knew his seven-year-old niece Ivy would like Emma. Ivy liked everyone. And Belle and Emma shared a common baby bond. It was Harlan he worried about, even though they had already met. And he hadn't been concerned up until his conversation with Wes yesterday morning. Granted, a lot had changed between him and Emma since then, but Wes's concern that Dylan was repeating old patterns bothered him. He didn't see any similarity between Emma and Lauren, but Wes had. Now he wondered if Harlan would, too.

Ivy greeted them before Emma had a chance to step out of the truck. "You're having a baby, just like Belle!" The little girl danced in front of them on the snow-packed drive. "Do you know if it's going to be a boy or girl?"

"It's a girl." Emma shared in Ivy's enthusiasm.

"Do you have a name yet?"

"Not yet. But I have to choose one soon."

"You could always name her Ivy." His niece grabbed hold of Emma's hand and led her through the back gate of his brother's white clapboard farmhouse. "Dad, Belle! Emma is having a baby!"

"Ivy, use your inside voice," Harlan warned from the top of the porch steps.

"But I'm outside," she protested.

Harlan rolled his eyes and stretched out his arm. "See what you have to look forward to? It's nice to see you under better circumstances. You look much better than the last time I saw you."

"Yeah, about that." Emma grimaced. "I'm sorry I screamed and cursed all the way to the hospital. I'm surprised I didn't shatter your eardrums."

"No worries. I've heard much worse. I'm just glad you're okay." Harlan slapped Dylan on the back. "Hey, man. You actually look a little more relaxed since I last saw you."

"Is Emma having your baby?" Ivy asked.

"Enough," Harlan warned again. "Why don't you take Elvis for a walk?

"Come on in." Harlan held the door open for them. "Belle will be down in a minute or two."

"Here I am." His sister-in-law pulled Emma into an all-encompassing hug. Dylan didn't know Emma well enough to know if she was the hug-everyone-you-meet type or not. Belle hadn't been until her pregnancy. "How far along are you?" Belle wrapped her arm around Emma's shoulder and steered her into the living room.

"Well, that's the last we'll see of them until dinner." Harlan opened the fridge and handed Dylan a beer. "What's going on? Wes told me you and your arch enemy have gotten pretty hot and heavy."

"I wouldn't say she's the enemy, anymore. I think we've come to an understanding." Dylan twisted the top off his beer and flicked the cap into the garbage can. "She knows I'm not going to sell."

"Does she?" Harlan asked.

"Yeah, why?"

Harlan shook his head. "It's nothing."

"No, if you have something to say, say it."

"Did you know Emma was in town today?" Harlan asked.

Dylan nodded. "She was buying things for the baby and Billy Johnson's kids."

"Okay." Harlan opened the oven door and peeked in. "Honey, you may want to check the lasagna. It's looking a little brown on top."

"I'll be right there," Belle called from the living room.

Dylan held up his arms. "You can't leave me hanging. What are you not telling me?"

"Get out of the way, you two." Belle swatted at them. "Pregnant woman coming through. This room isn't big enough for all of us and my belly."

Emma laughed from the doorway. "Wait until you reach thirty-three weeks. And I hear we get even bigger."

"I wouldn't mind so much if I didn't have to pee every two seconds."

"Really?" Harlan looked at Belle. "We're getting

ready to eat and you're talking about your bathroom habits."

"What habits? I made a statement, that's all." Belle opened the oven and quickly closed it. "Okay, dinner's ready. Here." She thrust two potholders at Harlan's chest. "You can take it out."

"Did you know, I'm her new manservant?"

"And he's not too happy about it. The doctor doesn't want me around any animal urine so that means this one here has to clean up after all my little ones at the rescue center when my volunteers aren't available."

"I'm sorry, that cow is not little. Neither is your three-hundred pound pig."

Emma laughed at Belle and Harlan's banter, but Dylan couldn't help wondering what his brother wasn't telling him about Emma. She hadn't mentioned going anywhere else in town, not that he expected her to report to him. She was free to go where she wanted. Still, something was amiss and he was going to find out before they left tonight.

EMMA COULDN'T FIGURE out what had changed between the time they arrived and the time they sat down to eat. Dylan had barely said two words throughout their meal. He'd glanced at her a few times, almost questioningly. Their tension began to make her feel uncomfortable and she could see the uncertainty in Belle's face as she wondered what was going on, as well. She was fairly certain Dylan had bad-mouthed her in the past, but they were past that now, weren't they?

Dylan and Harlan retired into the living room after dinner while Emma helped Belle clean up the kitchen. She had tried to hear what they were saying, but couldn't make out a word.

"Emma, please sit down. You don't have to help me. Your feet must be killing you at this stage."

"They were until I bought bigger boots. When I got here, I actually had to borrow somebody else's. No one told me my feet were going to get bigger during this whole process." Emma waved her hands in front of her belly. "And names. How do you choose a name for your child?"

"Tell me about it. How many names do you have on your list?" Belle asked. "I have hundreds and I can't manage to narrow them down. It doesn't help that we're waiting until the birth to find out the sex."

Emma shook her head. "I don't even have two."

Belle stared at her. "You have one name on your list? Doesn't that make it really easy then?"

"No, because I keep second-guessing it. I liked it and now I hate it, but I haven't come up with anything else."

"Whatever you do, don't ask Dylan for baby name advice. If he's anything like Harlan it will be something off-the-wall like Aloysius."

"Aloysius?"

Belle's brows furrowed. "It was some great-great uncle of theirs from way back when. Harlan said it was unusual enough to stand out and not worry about another kid in class having the same name."

"No doubt," Emma agreed. "Can I ask you something just between us?" Belle didn't owe Emma any loyalty, but she needed a logical explanation to explain Dylan's sudden mood change.

"Sure, go ahead."

"Dylan... Does he tend to—how should I put this?"

"Brood?"

Emma sagged against the counter. "Yes." She lowered her voice. "Exactly that."

"I've known him for almost my entire life, and the man he is today is much more jaded than he used to be. He tends to see the negative before the positive. It's my understanding you've already seen that side of him."

"That's an understatement." After the heartfelt talk he had with her stomach this morning, she had thought they had turned a new corner in their relationship. She still didn't know how to define it, although Dylan had hinted about making things official. Official as in dating. At least that's what she thought he meant. Because he couldn't possibly mean marriage. That was out of the question this early in the relationship. She didn't even know if they had a chance of dating past New Year's, let alone walk down the aisle. She didn't want to spend two seconds to say "I do" and then have to spend two years trying to say "I don't" in divorce court. At least that's what some of her coworkers had told her about their marriages.

"I'd like to tell you to take things day-by-day with him, but I know you two are pushing time. That is, unless you decide to move to Saddle Ridge."

"Let me get through this pregnancy first." Why did everyone make it sound so easy?

Emma filled Belle in on her Braxton-Hicks scare until Dylan and Harlan joined them. Dylan refused to make eye contact with her as they said their goodbyes. What could possibly have happened? At this point, it wasn't just frustrating, it was annoying the hell out of her.

"Thank you both for having me." Emma nodded to Harlan and gave Ivy and Belle a hug goodbye. "And don't forget to send me that vegetarian lasagna recipe. It was really good."

"I will." Belle called from the porch. "You two should drive around town and see the Christmas lights while you're out. Only four more days until Santa comes."

"I'd love to see the lights."

Dylan wordlessly held the car door open for her as she eased onto the seat. She was about to open her mouth to ask him if they could drive around for a while before heading back to the ranch when he closed the door. So much for that conversation.

Emma may be relatively new to town, but she knew her way around. The way they were heading home was definitely the most direct route and not to see any Christmas lights.

"Okay, Scrooge. Do you mind telling me what happened back there? You were fine when we arrived and then you weren't."

"Is there something you want to tell me?" he asked.

"Like what?"

"Like, I don't know, maybe how you went into town today and pulled the plats on my ranch and Barnaby Holcomb's. I can understand you pulling the plats on my land, although you should have them already. At least your office should. But Barnaby's? I'm sure he'll find out about that. This is a small town and news like that spreads faster than green grass through a goose."

Emma didn't know what to say. She clasped her hands on her belly and faced forward. If he could get this judgmental without discussing it with her then they had a problem.

"I guess it's true, then."

"You tell me. You seem to have already made up your mind."

"I had told you I wasn't going to sell. So why would you do that? It puts me in a really bad position."

"Because it's my job, Dylan. I spoke to Charlie earlier and he asked me to pull the plats on the Holcomb ranch so he could see the land survey. It doesn't matter if you were planning to sell or not. I'm not just answering to Charlie. I have to answer to a group of investors. If it goes south, I have to detail the reasons why and what I did to prevent it. Just be glad I'm the one here from my firm. They are already clamoring to take my place. You thought I pressured you? They would've swarmed like vultures around you."

"No, they wouldn't have. I would've thrown them off my ranch. Just like I—"

Emma snapped her head in his direction. "Just like you what? Should've done with me?"

"No. I was going to say just like I had tried to do with you." He tugged off his gloves and adjusted the heat. "I feel like a damned fool taking you to my brother's house and then hearing that."

Emma began to feel lightheaded. She inhaled deeply and exhaled slowly, trying her best not to raise her voice. "How do you think I feel knowing I sat at your brother's table and neither one of you trusted me?" The thought alone made her feel sick. "You both made me feel about as welcome as a skunk in church."

"How can we have a relationship if there isn't any trust?"

"We can't. So let's put it all out there." Emma fought against her seat belt in an attempt to gain more air. "You're only mad at me because if Barnaby Holcomb hears I pulled the plats on both lands he'll think I did it for you. And you don't want anything to jeopardize that offer, do you? Why didn't you tell me you received another bid on the ranch?"

"I knew it. How did you find out?" Dylan pulled into the supermarket parking lot and shifted the Wagoneer into Park. "I haven't even discussed that with anyone."

She unbuckled the blasted restraint and turned to him. "I overheard you and that man talking when I snowshoed out to the stables yesterday. Seriously, Dylan, if you don't want people listening in, I suggest you hold your meetings in a more private place like…oh, I don't know…maybe your house or your office. I waited over twenty-four hours for you to tell me about that offer and you haven't said a word. You probably still wouldn't have unless I brought it up."

"I didn't tell you because I haven't made a decision. It's a nice offer to fall back on, but it's not exactly what I had in mind. I would have preferred a partnership with Barnaby instead of relinquishing control of Silver Bells, but it was an all-or-nothing deal. I still have so many ideas for the ranch. I'm not ready to give it up."

"What if I said you could have your dream ranch?"

His icy laugh crackled between them. "Did I suddenly win a lottery I don't remember entering?"

"My firm has increased their offer by $100,000 and will guarantee employment for all current employees. While it won't be immediate employment at Silver Bells, we are willing to pay relocation fees if they want to work at one of our other investment groups resorts anywhere in the world."

"You're kidding, right?"

"Nope." Emma couldn't see how he could refuse the offer when it gave him the freedom to build whatever he wanted. "It would be a great opportunity for them. And you could buy your dream guest ranch here or elsewhere. You don't have to split the money with anyone and with the extra hundred grand, your options just increased exponentially. Imagine the possibilities."

"How can you preach to me about honesty? When were you planning to tell me this? After I told you about my offer?"

"My boss had asked me to tell you last night and get back to him today with your answer."

"So why didn't you?" Dylan rubbed the sleeve of his jacket against the fogged window.

"Because you invited me over for dinner and to decorate the Christmas tree in your uncle's memory. I wanted to honor him as well without ruining the moment with business."

Dylan's shoulders sagged and Emma believed she was finally getting through to him. "Fair enough. But I still don't understand why you pulled the plats. Oh, my God, they want Barnaby's ranch, too, don't they? Or was his a consolation prize in case I didn't sell?"

"It was a combination of both. If you don't sell and we present the investors with equally suitable land, the deal will remain intact. Just with different owners. And if you sold to us, we would try to purchase his land and expand the original design."

"And you would get your promotion."

"Yes, I would, but it wasn't about that."

"Whose idea was it to go after Barnaby's land? Yours or your boss's?" Dylan asked.

"I presented the idea and Charlie gave the go-ahead to pursue it." Emma swallowed and patted her belly. The butter bean was beginning to rock and roll inside her and Emma wasn't sure how much longer she could stand the pressure. "You should be happy. In the end, you're getting what you want. You never wanted to sell in the first place."

"This is about you being honest with me, Emma.

At least now we know neither one of us has been completely honest with the other."

Emma waved her fingers at the car keys. "Hey, the butter bean's not too fond of our conversation. We need to get back to the ranch."

"Are you all right?" Dylan started the engine and shifted into gear before taking her hand. "Do you need me to drive you to the hospital?"

"No." She continued to breathe. "It's just Braxton-Hicks again. I know what it feels like this time around."

"If you're sure?"

"Just drive, Dylan." Why did men always have to argue when you needed them to do something? "You still haven't answered me. What about my offer? It's pretty substantial."

"You seriously want to talk about this now?"

"As long as we both stay calm, we might as well get this over with once and for all. You've heard my final offer. What's your final answer?"

"It was never about the money," Dylan said under his breath.

"No, I thought it was about your employees. We're offering them a tremendous opportunity, and you're refusing to give them the chance to even consider it. I could understand if after you had sat down with them, put it on the table and *they* said no. But for you to make that decision for them…" Emma shook her head. "That tells me this was about your stubborn pride from the beginning."

DYLAN PARKED AS close to the lodge's entrance as he possibly could. Before he could get out of the Wagoneer, Emma had opened her door and was testing her ability to stand.

"Here, let me help you to your room." Dylan gripped her firmly by the elbow.

"I'm fine." She shrugged out of his grasp. "Please just go home and leave me alone. You bring out the contractions in me. I've had enough for one night."

"I'll let Sandy know what's going on so she can check on you."

Emma swatted goodbye over her shoulder as if he were a mosquito she was trying to kill. "Don't call me, I'll call you."

He understood Emma's annoyance, considering he was once again the reason she was in this condition. Nonetheless, he watched her through the glass doors as she made her way up the stairs and to her room. He tugged his phone from his jacket pocket and punched in Sandy's number. He knew she was busy with her wedding plans, but he needed someone to check in on Emma during the night and there was no way she'd allow him anywhere near her. Which was fine by him. They needed some distance.

After speaking with Sandy, he called Melinda for good measure. And then he called Harlan to fill him in on the details. He loved his brother dearly, but Harlan may have overreacted a tad to the situation, which in turn had damaged Dylan's relationship with Emma. He couldn't blame his brother for being suspicious. It was his nature as an officer of the law to question everything, but neither one of them had had the facts. He couldn't fault Emma for doing her job. He may not like it, but it was her job and he had known that before they got involved. He couldn't expect her to put her livelihood behind his.

He'd been an ass. And a first-class one at that. He needed to make it up to her, and there was only one way he knew how. He unlocked the front door of the house, flicked on the lights and tore through the stacks of paperwork on the kitchen table until he found it. The drawing he had sketched of the rocking horse for Emma's baby. And on the back, a cradle. He may never have the opportunity to see the butter bean use them, but he wanted her to have something special that he had made with his own two hands.

Dylan ran back down the front porch stairs, almost wiping out in the process. He drove the Wagoneer farther down the road to his log cabin, and pulled around back near the woodshop. Christmas was in four days, technically three once midnight rolled around. Both were fairly basic designs, but he needed to start now, if he planned to have them finished by then. That is, if she didn't pack up and leave in the morning. There weren't many hotel-type places to stay in town. But Whitefish and Kalispell weren't far and he was sure they'd have vacancies available. Then he ran the risk of never seeing her again. And he couldn't bear the thought.

Dylan ran his hands over a couple pieces of mahogany he had set aside for a special project. He didn't know what could be more special than Emma's baby. He already missed the butter bean and they hadn't even met yet. Hopefully he'd still have that chance.

Chapter Twelve

Christmas Eve morning rolled around and Emma had managed to evade Dylan since their argument. He hadn't seen a single sign of her around the lodge and had even questioned Sandy if she was still staying there. Her rental hadn't moved from where she'd last parked it days ago. After Luke told him Emma had been avoiding the dining room because of him, he began eating at home so she could freely mingle with everyone else.

He understood and respected her reasons, but it was Christmas Eve. Nobody should be alone on Christmas Eve. His brother Garrett and his two children would be arriving soon. Harlan, Belle and Ivy were joining them for dinner and even Wes agreed to make an appearance. It was as close to complete as their family could get with Ryder being in jail and his mom in California with her new husband.

Bracing himself for an onslaught, he knocked lightly on Emma's door. When she didn't answer, he knocked again. Still no answer. He figured either she wasn't there or she had seen him through the peephole and refused to acknowledge him.

Unwilling to give up that easily, Dylan thought of the one thing that would get her to open the door. He took a few steps back and started to sing at the top of his lungs, "Oh what fun it is to ride in a one-horse open sleigh!"

He heard Emma fumble with the lock before swinging the door wide. "Are you crazy? Keep your voice down. The situation is bad enough. I don't need you telling everyone what we did."

"You mean that we made love on a sleigh under a moonlit sky. Sounds pretty romantic to me." Dylan scanned the length of her body, reassuring himself she was okay.

"Hey, cowboy, my eyes are up here."

"Can I come in?"

Emma stepped aside. "Why not? You own the place."

For someone who hadn't been out of the hotel for days, she'd certainly been busy. Neatly wrapped packages lined the wall next to the bed. Numerous pink and blue bags sat next to the bed along with new soft pink luggage.

"Where did you get all of this stuff?"

"I picked up a few things here and in Kalispell."

"But your car hasn't moved."

Emma's left brow rose. "What did you do, draw a chalk outline around it? I haven't been driving. I don't trust myself in case I get one of those Braxton-Hicks contractions again."

"Who's been your chauffeur?"

"Well, if you must know, yesterday I went into town with Melinda and Rhonda, and other days I called for car service. What is the big deal?"

Here, Dylan thought she'd been cooped up in a room avoiding him and she'd been out having a good time. Which was great for her, it just made him feel like a complete and total idiot.

"I didn't realize you were going out. I thought you were staying in your room because of me."

"Don't flatter yourself. No man is ever worth locking yourself in a room and pining over."

Emma certainly didn't keep her feelings to herself.

"I know you are still mad at me and I can't blame you. It's Christmas Eve, and I would like to invite you to celebrate with my family. They will all be here tonight and despite what happened with Harlan, who feels bad about the situation, I think you would have a good time with us. We are loud and fun, a little quirky, but most importantly we all believe there's always room for one more at the table. Besides, I have another reason for asking you."

Emma sat on the edge of the bed, looking as uncomfortable as the day was long. "What is your reason?"

"Jax used to play Santa for all the kids on the ranch. Since he's no longer here, I'm playing Santa, and I was hoping you would be my Mrs. Claus. I asked Sandy, but she's too busy getting ready for the wedding. Unless you're not up to it."

Emma seemed more pregnant than she had a few

days ago. He'd always heard about women popping in the weeks leading up to the delivery, and he wondered if this was what they meant.

"Are you all right?"

"I'm just tired. I overdid it yesterday. What time do you need me to play Mrs. Claus?"

"Not until after dinner. I'm honoring the tradition and hosting it at Jax's house. We have more than enough food, especially since I didn't make it. The chefs here did. It's very casual and I would love to see you there."

Emma studied him for a second or two, making him think she'd say no. "Where am I supposed to find a Mrs. Claus costume?"

"Oh, we have one. The woman who used to play Mrs. Claus quit over the summer." Dylan held up his hands. "And before you ask, yes, you will fit into it. It's very loose fitting."

"Okay."

"Okay to which part?" Dylan wanted her to say yes to both, but his heart couldn't afford to get his hopes up. Just being in the same room with her knowing she despised him was agony.

"Both, if someone's willing to pick me up and drive me back."

"And by someone I am assuming you mean someone other than me."

Emma shifted on the bed so both of her legs were outstretched in front of her. "I will ride with you, providing you behave yourself."

It was a start, and he was thrilled to have the chance to try and set things right between them.

"I will pick you up out front around 4:30, if that's okay."

"Good, then I can nap until three." Emma rolled on to her side, and he longed to spoon her as he had the night of their sleigh ride. "Can you lock the door behind you, please?"

The sound of her breathing had changed from normal to deep before his hand reached the knob. She was already asleep. He allowed himself the pleasure of watching her for a few seconds before leaving. She was beautifully strong and fragile in the same breath, and he already missed her more than he should.

EMMA AWOKE TO the sound of her text message tone. It was Sunday so nobody from work should be bothering her. She reached for her phone and saw Dylan's name on the screen. Wasn't it enough that she had agreed to spend the evening with him and his family? She just hoped this time went better than the last. Besides, she'd already met three of the Slade men, she might as well make it an even four. She tapped the screen to display his message.

Just a friendly wake-up text since you hadn't set your alarm before you fell asleep.

Had she really fallen asleep while he was there? She replayed his visit in her mind, unable to remember him leaving. Well, that had been incredibly rude of her. Even Dylan didn't deserve that.

Dylan didn't deserve most of what she'd been dishing out. She hadn't been avoiding him because she was mad. A bit miffed, but not mad. She had kept her distance to maintain her sanity and protect her heart. She couldn't believe some of the things she'd done. Namely sleeping with a virtual stranger. But even more so, she couldn't believe some of the things she'd almost done. Like contemplating partnering with him on the ranch. She needed to have her head examined for all of the above. If she had been one of her friends, she'd be extremely worried about them. Which was why she hadn't filled Jennie in on any of the juicier Dylan details. Her recklessness embarrassed her, but dammit if she didn't miss him.

Dressed and downstairs by half past four, she was surprised when Belle pulled in front of the lodge instead of Dylan. She tried telling herself it eliminated the pressure of being alone with him in the car, but even she couldn't deny the fact she was disappointed. Belle was great company, though and if she lived in town, they'd probably be fast friends.

Emma could hear little kids screeching from inside Jax's house the moment she stepped out of Belle's truck. At least hers was a relatively normal height off the ground.

"Are you ready for this?" Belle asked. "Because I'm not sure if I am."

"Why not?" Emma was surprised to see Belle hesitate at the front door. "This is my first Christmas with the Slades since I was a teenager. I haven't seen Garrett since my first wedding to Harlan, which was a no-go because he left me at the altar."

"Harlan left you at the altar? And you married him anyway?" And she thought she and Dylan had problems.

"I let him suffer for eight years before we tried it again. It's a long story. Remind me to tell you about it someday."

"Here I thought I was the only nervous one tonight." Emma peered through the window on the other side of the door. "I'll tell you what. You have my back and I'll have yours."

"You have a deal." The women shook on it before walking into the madhouse known as the Slade family Christmas.

"I'm glad you made it." Dylan kissed her lightly on the cheek. "I had my doubts you would show up."

"I'm curious to see how the other half lives."

"The other half?"

"My parents never did much for the holidays. Don't get me wrong, we had a good time and it was special, but it wasn't anything like this." She couldn't imagine children and pets running around her parents' townhouse, or people eating off paper plates and drinking out of red plastic cups. "We celebrated Christmas, but the tree went up and came down within a matter of days. When I was home for the holidays, it was just my parents and myself since I'm an only child."

"You don't have any other family?"

"I have family scattered across the country, but

none that live in Illinois. My father moved there for his hospital residency and they never left. Then I came along."

"Thank God for small favors."

"Ha!" Emma laughed so hard, she thought the butter bean would make an appearance. "A week ago you thought I was the worst person on earth."

"I wouldn't exactly say the worst." Ivy ran between them followed by another little girl and boy. "That's Kacey and Bryce, my brother Garrett's two kids. Kacey's seven and Bryce is four. Let me introduce you."

DYLAN HADN'T SEEN Emma laugh since, well, ever. And when she did, she cried. Actual tears. Harlan had taken her aside shortly after her arrival and apologized for meddling in her business. Between the children's fascination with her and Belle's baby bellies and Ivy's dog Elvis's fixation on Emma's plate, the woman barely managed a mouthful here and there. None of it appeared to bother her. Except when it came time to sing *Jingle Bells*. Emma turned a brilliant red every time they sang the line "Oh what fun it is to ride in a one-horse open sleigh."

Their magical moonlight romp would forever remain their secret and their secret alone. Dylan couldn't imagine spending that moment with anyone other than Emma. It would forever remain his favorite memory of all time. He didn't think anything could possibly beat it.

When the children were busy playing near the large stone fireplace, Dylan motioned for Emma to follow him into the bedroom. He had both of their costumes hidden in the back of the closet for fear the little ones would stumble across them during a game of hide-and-seek. While he was sure Bryce still believed in Santa, he wasn't so sure he could fool Kacey and Ivy. Especially Ivy, since he spent the most time around her.

Dylan closed the door behind them, giving them a moment alone while they changed. "Um, I didn't think this part through." He turned and faced the corner. "You go ahead. I'll stay here and give you your privacy."

"I appreciate it, but it's not necessary. When you're pregnant, you lose your inhibitions about people seeing you in various stages of undress real quick. Besides, you're probably going to have to help me get these bloomer things on. I wasn't expecting this intricate of a costume."

Dylan faced Emma who had managed to get her head and one arm into Mrs. Claus's dress before realizing it had a zipper down the back. "Oh crap! Help me already."

"Stop flailing around like a catfish on a dock." Dylan lowered the zipper and eased the red and white apron dress over her curves. "See, that wasn't so bad."

"For you. Why do I have two pairs of bloomers? You just have to put on pants and a jacket."

"If I remember correctly, one pair of bloomers is shorter than the other to allow for the dress to pouf out."

"Oh, sure. That's just what I need. To look even

pouffier than I already do." Emma eyed his bare abs as he tugged off his shirt. "Let me tell you something, Santa. You better shove a pillow or two under that jacket so I don't look like roly-poly Mrs. Claus."

Dylan stepped into the red velour pants and adjusted the suspenders. "I think you make a sexy Mrs. Claus." He braved a quick peck on her lips.

"I think you've been sipping too much eggnog." Emma attempted to step into the second pair of bloomers and almost fell onto the bed. "See, I told you."

Dylan picked the bloomers up off the floor and knelt before her. He widened one leg opening and held it out for her to step into before doing the same with the other. He eased the white cotton up her thighs before settling them on her hips. The costume may be corny, but the intimacy left him wanting more. The swell of her belly and breasts pressed against him, her lips inches from his own. He wanted to brand her with his mouth and claim her body and soul before she had a chance to leave him again.

"Santa?" A soft rap emanated from the other side of the door, interrupting the moment. "It's me, Belle. I have the naughty and nice list."

Dylan unlocked the door. Belle eased it open with one hand over her eyes. "Okay you two, put your clothes back on."

"Ha, ha. Very funny. I'll have you know I'm wearing two pairs of bloomers. Santa can't get through these."

"You wanna bet?" Dylan sidled up next to her until

she swatted him away. "Hey, Belle, why do you look so frazzled? Are the kids getting the best of you?"

"There are so many of them."

"There's three," Emma laughed.

"Yes, but when they're together, it's like they multiply." Belle collapsed on the bed. "You two go without me. Tell everyone I'm guarding Santa's sleigh. They'll understand."

"Oh no you don't." Emma grabbed her hand and began pulling her off the bed. "You're not sending me in there without backup."

"Dylan's your backup. I'm pooped."

"Come on, Belle." He reached for her other hand. "Someone has to distract the kids while we sneak outside."

"Outside?" Emma and Belle said in unison.

"It's cold out there. You hadn't mentioned anything about going outside in my bloomers when I agreed to this."

"Okay, fine." One pregnant woman was enough, let alone two. "Belle, you just distract them and we'll pretend we came in from outside. When you're ready just say something like, *Do I hear Santa Claus?* And we'll take it from there."

They turned out the bedroom lights and waited in the darkness for Belle's signal. Even a white-haired wig and wire-rimmed glasses couldn't abate the feelings he had for Emma. He just hoped her jovial mood continued until tomorrow morning, because he had a special surprise planned for her and the butter bean.

"Did you hear that?" Belle said from the living

room. "I think I heard reindeer on the roof. Who wants to run upstairs and check it out for me?"

"I will, I will," the kids shouted. They waited until they heard tiny footsteps on the staircase before emerging from the bedroom.

"Ho, ho, ho!" Dylan belted in his deepest voice as he and Emma walked toward the fireplace.

"We probably should've put the fire out before we did this. They're never going to believe we came down that thing." Emma squeezed beside him. "Ho, ho, ho!" She leaned closer and asked, "Mrs. Claus says, 'ho, ho, ho,' right?"

"Every time she catches Santa at the strip joint," Wes offered. "Be careful you don't set your bloomers on fire."

Belle started to laugh. "Then we can call you hotpants."

Emma stuck her tongue out.

"Who's been naughty and who's been nice?" Dylan chuckled in his best Santa impression.

"I swear to God," Emma said with a hiss. "If any of you say anything, I'll make sure there's a lump of coal in your stocking tomorrow morning."

At least they were all laughing when the kids clambered down the stairs. After twenty minutes of beard pulling, questions about reindeer poop and Elvis almost attacking his jingle bells, Dylan had enough Santa for the year.

Once they had changed and the kids were tucked into their beds for the night, Dylan drove Emma back to the lodge and walked her to her door.

"Thank you for inviting me tonight. I really enjoyed spending time with your family."

"The pleasure was all mine. Thank you for letting this rift between us go for the holiday."

"Maybe peace on earth could spread past tomorrow." Emma looked up at him. "I would love to ask you in, but I'm afraid I don't have the strength or the stamina to give you what you want."

Dylan took her hand in his and lifted it to his mouth, kissing the top of it. "The only thing I want is your happiness. Merry Christmas, Emma." His lips brushed hers in a brief yet tender kiss. "I'll see you in the morning."

"Merry Christmas, Dylan. Thank you for making tonight special."

Dylan felt like he was walking on air by the time he reached the lobby. After three days of silence, he finally felt hopeful again. His Christmas wish: a lifetime with Emma and her daughter.

Chapter Thirteen

Christmas morning, Emma awoke happier than she had been in years. After watching Dylan with the children last night, she had fallen asleep wondering what it would be like if he were her daughter's father. She had missed Dylan more than she'd been willing to admit, and after spending time with him and his family, she wasn't too eager to go back to the way things were.

She assumed she would hate the silence of the country. She had lived in the city for so long, the twenty-four-hour bustle had become second nature. But the Montana silence had grown on her and she actually found it quite relaxing. It wasn't all tranquility, though. She loved Dylan's brand of loud. Children playing, brothers arguing good-naturedly, a sister-in-law clearly not ready to have a baby. She wanted it all. And she wanted it by Dylan's side.

He still hadn't given Emma an answer to her final proposal. At least she wouldn't accept their last conversation about it as a final answer. That would determine her next course of action.

Or, would it?

She didn't need Dylan's answer to decide if she wanted to make a new life in Montana. It didn't matter either way. Dylan was here. Granted, he could always sell the ranch and move to Wyoming. He had mentioned it once. So what? She could go with him. The spark was still there between them. She had felt the passion last night without the physical touch or the words. Although, she certainly wouldn't thumb her nose at those.

Her parents would probably die of humiliation and her friends would probably try to have her committed, because moving to Montana was insane.

Absolutely...the best idea she'd had in a long time.

Emma's phone dinged. She checked her messages only to find one from Luke. He was heading over to see Billy Johnson's family this morning and said he would take the gifts she'd bought. She originally wanted to bring them there herself then she decided it was best if they were anonymous, the same with the donation her company gave them. Charlie hadn't seen it that way, but he reluctantly agreed. She hadn't spoken to the office since Friday, after agreeing to reconvene on Tuesday morning. She already dreaded it. One more reason to move to Montana.

She had hoped to hear from Dylan since he had mentioned having a surprise for her. She couldn't wait to see what it was. Although, she didn't have anything for him and certainly didn't expect a gift.

Someone began knocking jingle bells against her door. She flew to it, well, as fast as a woman with twenty-five extra pounds and swollen feet could, and threw the door open.

"Luke, it's only you." She stepped aside so he could enter the room.

"Merry Christmas to you, too."

"I'm sorry, Merry Christmas." She gave him a hug. "I didn't mean to be rude. When you knocked that way I just assumed you were Dylan."

"I haven't seen him yet this morning. Did you get my message? I'm ready to take those packages over to the Johnsons."

"They're right here." Emma waved her arm at the wall. She had originally bought a few things for the children then decided his wife deserved gifts, too.

Luke removed his hat and placed it over his heart. "My word, are these all for the Johnson family?"

Emma hoped she didn't offend anyone with the number of gifts. Due to her predicament, they were the only ones she'd purchased this year. "Yes, they are."

"And you're sure you don't want them to know they came from you."

"Considering the role I played in all of this, I think it's best." Emma enjoyed playing secret Santa and made a vow to adopt a family every year from now on.

"You have a big heart. Thank you." Luke set his hat back atop his head and looked around. "This might take a few trips."

"I can help you bring some of them down."

"You will do no such thing." Luke ushered her toward the door. "Leave me your room key, and I will bring these downstairs while you grab some breakfast before the French toast is all gone."

"Sounds like a plan. The key is on the dresser. I'll see you a little later."

"Oh, and, Emma, you might want to bring your coat and gloves. It's a bit chilly down there this morning. Something's wrong with the heat."

"Okay, thanks. That's kind of rough on Christmas day. The rest of the lodge will stay warm, won't it?"

"Sure. The dining and great room are on a separate system."

Emma slipped on her coat and jammed her gloves in the pockets. If it was too cold, she'd bring her breakfast back to the room. No sense in freezing when she didn't need to.

"Merry Christmas," one of the guests said as they passed her in the hallway.

That was odd. They weren't wearing their coats. As she descended the stairs overlooking the great room, she noticed nobody had a coat on. "What was Luke talking about?"

And then she saw him. Dylan walked through the glass doors and met her at the foot of the stairs. "Good morning, beautiful." He kissed the back of her hand. "And Merry Christmas. Your chariot awaits." He swept his arm to the side, revealing a double-row red sleigh with a team of two Belgian draft horses parked in front of the lodge.

"Merry Christmas." She bounced up and down. "What have you done?"

He held the door open for her. "You're about to find out."

Emma attempted to peek into the second row of the sleigh, but Dylan caught her mid-act. "Everything is covered up back there so you're wasting your time."

She settled beneath the sleigh's blankets, eager to see what he had planned next. Maybe it was the slight drop in the overnight temperature or the magic of Christmas, but Emma swore everything twinkled, from the trees to the ground itself as the sleigh glided across the snow. They stopped at their special place overlooking Saddle Ridge. Even the town sparkled in the morning light.

Dylan reached behind them and lifted a large insulated picnic basket. "This morning we dine alfresco." He sat the basket on the floor. "I will have you know, I had to look up that word just for this occasion."

He withdrew two insulated mugs and handed one to her before setting his on the floor. "Homemade hot chocolate, made by yours truly." And then he handed her a large covered insulated plate. He removed the cover revealing a piping hot stack of French toast with a side of maple syrup. "Also made by yours truly."

"I can't believe you did all of this. Not even in my wildest dreams could I have envisioned breakfast on a horse-drawn sleigh. You truly are a man of many talents."

Dylan smiled at her. "Oh, you have no idea."

After they ate, Emma enjoyed snuggling with Dylan beneath the layers of blankets as the sun warmed their faces. His strong arms enveloped her, making her feel safe and secure against the uncertainty of tomorrow. This was what she wanted. She knew every day wouldn't be French toast and sleigh rides. And that was okay. It was the company of the man beside her that made it special.

She rested her head against his shoulders and sighed at the serenity that had become her new norm. "I never want to leave this place."

Dylan nuzzled his face against her hair. "Neither do I, but I have another surprise for you."

Every inch of her body tingled in anticipation. "You've already done so much. What more could you possibly have planned?"

"Do you want to find out?"

Emma twisted to look in the seat behind them. "Yes, yes I do." Emma thought her face would crack from smiling so big.

"It's not back there. It's waiting for you someplace else." Dylan took hold of the reins and clucked the horses forward.

The majestic beauty of the wide-open spaces nestled between the Swan Range and Mission Mountains was enough to bring tears to her eyes. How could she have ever wanted to take this away from Dylan? Her heart ached knowing she had hurt the man she loved. And yes, she loved Dylan Slade. She felt it all the way down to the tips of her toes.

Up ahead in the distance, Emma saw a large golden package shimmering against the pure white snowy backdrop. As they drew closer, the package appeared even larger. Dylan steered the sleigh alongside it and

Emma couldn't believe her eyes. It had to be at least a four-foot square box with a gigantic white bow on top.

"How in the world did you get this out here?" Emma ran her hands across the gold foil paper, testing its rigidity.

"I had a little help from Wes. I wanted to do something special and completely unexpected. I'm pretty sure this will be another *first* you can add to your list." He slid out from under the blankets and walked around to her side of the sleigh. He offered her his hand as she stepped onto the snow. "I will need to help you with this."

Emma rested her hand on top of the package. "But I didn't get you anything."

Dylan laughed at her distress. "Honey, I have what I want for Christmas. You. That's enough for me. Now come on, let's open your present."

He lifted the box, revealing the most adorable rocking horse and cradle. Emma covered her mouth. She had never seen anything more beautiful. She ran her hands over the smooth wood, admiring the craftsmanship.

"I've never seen anything like these. They're absolutely beautiful." Emma wiped her eyes, unable to control her tears. "Where on earth—?"

"I made them."

"You what?"

"I made them for you and the butter bean. I would have liked to have given both of them more detail, but I only had a few days. They're made from solid mahogany so they'll last a lifetime and then some."

"But how?" Emma placed her hands on the seat of the horse, testing the perfectly arched rockers beneath it.

"I have a woodshop behind what's actually my house."

"They are impeccable." Emma patted her chest. "I am touched and honored that you took the time and effort to make something like this for me and my daughter. It's beyond generous."

Dylan closed the distance between them. "I wanted to give you both a part of me. I wanted you to know how special you both are. Every time you use the cradle, know that my hands once lay where your daughter's head rests. When she rocks and laughs on the horse, know I was smiling when I made it. This is my gift to you, to your child, because you both have come to mean so much to me in a short amount of time. Even if we never have tomorrow, know how truly blessed I feel to have had you in my life."

Emma didn't think it was possible to define true love, but Dylan had proved her wrong once again. His gift epitomized it. His words captured the very essence of the emotion. And Emma wanted nothing more than to share her child with somebody who truly loved her daughter as much as she did.

AFTER A PERFECT Christmas day, Emma agreed to be Dylan's date for Luke and Sandy's evening wedding ceremony. The soft touch of Emma's hand in his as his friends recited their vows caused him to yearn for the same permanence. His next marriage would be forever. His next marriage would be to Emma if he had anything to say about it.

Each time his plane had glided over the mahogany when he was creating the cradle, his love for Emma and her daughter had grown. He knew then, his life wouldn't be complete without them. He wanted them to live with him in Jax's house on the ranch. She had admittedly grown to love Saddle Ridge and he hoped it wouldn't take too much more coaxing to convince her to run the ranch by his side. That is if his idea went according to plan. It was a big if, but after hearing his brother Garrett last night once again talk about wanting to move, he may have found the solution he'd been searching for.

Emma joined him on the makeshift dance floor in the center of the lodge's great room. He sincerely hoped it wasn't the last wedding he'd witness on the ranch. He loved Emma's idea of an open-air wedding chapel overlooking Saddle Ridge. He'd already begun sketching it in his mind and wanted to build it with his own two hands, so when he said, "I do" to Emma someday down the road, it would be even more special.

"Penny for your thoughts." Emma gazed up at him as they swayed to the music.

"I was thinking about your chapel idea."

"Imagine that. We can actually agree on something."

"I think we have managed to find common ground on quite a few things once we talked them out and understood where the other was coming from. You were right about my stubbornness. I didn't want to hear what you had to say."

"You don't have to say that. I'm ashamed to admit how many times I disregarded your feelings about the ranch. I realize now it's about much more than money. In my line of work, they teach us not to allow our emotions to interfere with the overall vision of a project. After six years of that, my humanity had all but disappeared. You helped me find it again."

Dylan felt a jolt against his lower abdomen. "What was that?" He froze, afraid to move.

"That was the butter bean." Emma smiled up at him.

"You're not going to tell me I bring out the contractions in you again, are you?"

Emma shook her head and laughed. "No, I'm not. This is normal baby behavior."

"It was strong. If that's what it felt like to me, I can only imagine what it does to your insides." Dylan led her off the dance floor and to the couch.

"Believe me when I tell you, the entire center of my body aches on a constant basis. I will be very happy when the next seven weeks are up."

He sat down beside her. "Would you mind?" He asked, pointing to her belly.

"Go right ahead."

Emma closed her eyes as his hands cupped the curve of her abdomen. He felt the ever slight motion of her daughter moving beneath his palms. It truly was a miracle. A tiny human was living and growing under his hands. The baby shifted again, causing

Emma to wince slightly. A more pronounced protrusion poked against him. He imagined it was the butter beans hand reaching out for his. *Soon, little one.* Regardless of where Emma had the baby, he'd find his way there.

"Still no name?"

"No. I read online that many mothers struggle finding the perfect name only to have it come to them the moment they see their child. I have resolved to wait at this point. If something comes to me before then, great. If not, I'm not going to stress over it."

"You've changed a lot over the past week."

"Has it only been a week? I feel like I've been here for an eternity. I don't mean that in a negative way." Emma rested her hand against his chest. "Between the year-long research and time I put into this ranch, I feel much more connected to it now than I had when I barged in here last week."

"I wouldn't exactly say you barged in."

"You're being too kind." She yawned. "I hate to be a party pooper, but I think I've reached my limit tonight."

Dylan rose and helped her to her feet. "I'll walk you to your room." He entwined his fingers with hers as they wished the bride and groom well. Dylan unlocked her door, wanting desperately to follow her inside and hold her in his arms until the sun came up tomorrow morning. But he couldn't. He had a week to save the ranch, and tonight he needed to talk to his brother before he left to go home to Wyoming tomorrow.

"Thank you for making this the most magical Christmas ever."

"I have enjoyed every moment I spent with you today. A week ago, I never thought I'd say that. You are a true joy and inspiration in my life and I look forward to tomorrow. I look forward to every day I'm with you. Merry Christmas, Emma."

"Merry Christmas, Dylan."

He kissed her goodbye before tearing himself away from her door. He had seen Garrett hovering near the buffet line and wanted to catch him before he took the kids back to the house and put them to bed.

Bryce and Kasey were dancing with Ivy and a few other ranch children in the center of the great room while his three brothers stood shoulder to shoulder watching them. Amazingly enough, Wes hadn't absconded with a bridesmaid.

"Got a minute for me to run something by you?" Dylan asked Garrett.

"Sure. What's on your mind?"

"I have a proposition for you," Dylan said.

"Uh-oh, don't do it, man. It's a sinking ship," Wes unnecessarily added.

"Let's talk in Jax's office where we won't be interrupted." Dylan led Garrett down the hallway.

"I have a feeling I know where this is going," Garrett said from behind.

"Before you form any opinions, hear me out. I have a few ideas you might really like, starting with a wedding chapel."

THE LAUGHTER AND celebrating downstairs kept Emma awake. After an hour, she gave up. She had always hated going home too soon for fear she'd miss out on something good happening at a party. She slipped into her leggings and an oversized sweater. She was sure nobody would mind her rejoining them wearing more comfortable attire. Maybe Dylan would still be there. And maybe there would still be cake. Because she always had room for cake. And maybe they still had one or two of those cheesy puffed pastries. She had room for those, too.

She wandered back toward the party and straight for the buffet. Jackpot. Cake and pastry. She fixed herself a plate and ate as she mingled, keeping an eye out for Dylan. When she spotted Harlan and Belle near the dance floor, she toe-tapped her way across the room. She felt a second wind coming on. Sometimes this happened at three o'clock in the morning. Tonight, it was a little earlier. She could handle earlier. It didn't disrupt her sleep.

"You didn't happen to see if there was any fruit salad left, did you?" Belle asked when she saw her plate.

Emma nodded as she took another mouthful and motioned to the buffet table with her fork.

"Harlan, would you be a dear and—"

"Big or little?"

"Big or little what?" Belle looked up at him.

"Do you want a big or a little bowl?"

Belle tilted her head and stared at him incredulously. "Do you even have to ask?"

"No, I sure didn't. I'll be right back."

"I thought you went to bed?" Belle said as Emma sat beside her on the couch.

"I attempted to. I figured if Dylan was still here, we could hang out for a bit and maybe even watch a movie in my room."

"He's still here. He's with Garrett in Jax's office. They've been in there ever since you left. Poke your head in and see how much longer they are going to be. Harlan and I want to get Ivy home and Garrett's two are getting sleepy."

"Okay, I'll nudge them along for you." Emma and her cake leisurely strolled down the hallway toward Jax's office. She had passed the black-and-white photos on the walls numerous times but had never taken a moment to look at them. The first few were from the early 1900s when they were building the lodge. Log structures had always fascinated her the way they notched and stacked each timber into position. By the time she reached the last photo, she had finished her cake.

"So what do you think?" She heard Dylan say. "Would you consider becoming my partner on the ranch and seeing if we can make a go of it? You keep telling me how much you want to get out of Wyoming. And you know everybody here."

Emma saw Garrett's reflection in the framed photo that hung on the wall opposite the office. "I think your ideas have some strong possibilities. The couples-only packages are a nice touch and I really like the chapel. Offering destination weddings would push

Silver Bells into an entirely different category. We can keep it rugged and Western, but still offer some elegance."

Emma couldn't believe it. Those were her ideas, some of which came from her buyout proposal. It shouldn't surprise her, though. He had come right out and told her he wanted to steal her ideas and use them to his advantage. She just didn't think he would, at least not without her.

"I wanted to run it past you before I asked Harlan and Wes if they wanted to buy in. Which I doubt they will, but I have to at least offer. I had also considered offering some of the employees a chance to own a part of the ranch. I think if we band together, we'd have a strong chance of competing with our neighboring guest ranches without becoming an over-the-top exclusive resort."

"I agree. Let's keep Silver Bells in the family."

"Congratulations. You found your solution. I'm glad you both liked my ideas." Emma stood in the open doorway of the office.

Garrett looked from Emma to Dylan. "These were your ideas?"

Emma bobbed her head. "Most of them, some of which I worked a year on developing. Dylan can tell you all about it. I wish you guys luck on your venture."

Emma stormed down the hallway as fast as her pregnant waddle would allow. She had made a mistake. A huge mistake and she couldn't get back home to Chicago quick enough.

"Emma, wait," Dylan called after her.

"Wait for what?" She spun on him. "Wait for you to steal more of my ideas?"

"You're right, they were your ideas. While my original intentions were to steal them, I gave your proposal serious thought. But in the end, it didn't make me want to sell. It made me want to hold on to the ranch even more."

"So you just decided to steal them?"

"I didn't realize they were copyrighted," Dylan retorted. "What's wrong with me implementing some of those ideas? They were good. You should feel flattered."

"Oh, sure. I feel really flattered. I'm the idiot who thought maybe, just maybe, I could run this ranch with you. I even—" Emma stomped down the hallway and back. "I even entertained the idea of becoming your partner. Because I believed in you. I saw how much this meant to you." She twisted her hair off her neck and held it up, suddenly very hot. "What was all this talk about wanting to have me by your side."

"I do want you by my side. I want you to stay here, with me. I thought I made that clear today."

"As what?" Emma sighed when he didn't answer. "I thought you wanted me as a partner."

"I did."

"Did?"

"A few days ago I had planned to ask you to stay and be the new lodge manager."

That wasn't quite the partner she had meant, but that had been part of it. "So why didn't you?"

"Because Barnaby presented me with his proposal a few hours later and I couldn't offer you something not knowing what I was going to do. So, I decided to wait until I had made up my mind."

"Until you made up your mind about the ranch or me?" Emma gave him one more opportunity to tell her how he felt about her.

"The ranch."

Emma waited for him to tell her he had already made up his mind about her, but he didn't. "Then where do I fit into all of this?"

"Honestly…" Dylan shrugged. "I don't know, anymore. I owe it to my brothers to ask them if they want to join in the venture. Until I have their answers, I have nothing to offer you. I had no idea you wanted to be this deeply involved in the ranch. You had already told me your daughter would be born in Chicago regardless of what happened between us. Why would I assume otherwise?"

Emma shook her head. "Because you asked me to stay this morning and I thought that meant something." Like maybe he loved her. "Well, you don't have to worry about it anymore. I will be out of your life soon enough."

"I don't understand why you're so upset."

"Because you left me with nothing. No promotion in Chicago and no job here in Montana. Yet, you and your brothers reap the benefits of my hard work. You cut me out of everything. And I'm still waiting for you to tell me you love me."

When Dylan didn't respond, Emma stormed back

to her room. She was a fool for ever believing they could have a perfect little Montana family.

It was over.

They were over.

Chapter Fourteen

Emma had a rough night. After hot sweats, minor contractions and a whole lot of pressure in new places, she phoned the doctor first thing in the morning. They told her to come in right away. Not wanting to bother anyone else on the ranch, she called for car service. On her way out the door, she saw Dylan and Garrett announce the ranch's new plans to the Silver Bells employees. She walked into the cold mountain air as they applauded and celebrated the news. In the end, Dylan had made the right decision and she was happy for the jobs he had saved.

Her exam left her craving the comforts of home. Chicago almost felt foreign to her and the lodge was nothing more than a room. When she said the actual word *home* aloud, Jax's house had immediately come to mind. It would take a long time for her to shake Dylan from her system.

"Emma?" Belle said from a chair in the waiting room. "Is everything all right?"

"How did you know I was here?" Emma asked.

"I didn't. This is my doctor. She doesn't have an office any place else. Just here."

"Oh." Emma sat down beside her. "Where's Harlan?"

"At work." Belle took her hand and gave it a squeeze. "What happened?"

"My blood pressure is back up and I'm almost two centimeters dilated. The baby has already dropped. Here, I thought I'd been experiencing another round of Braxton-Hicks when I noticed I wasn't carrying as high as I had been hours earlier. She gave me a round of steroid shots in preparation for an early delivery. Further travel is out, and I have been ordered to take it easy. Limited exercise, very short walks and no sex."

"You must be terrified."

"I am." Emma fought back the tears that threatened to break free. "The doctor estimates her at almost five pounds, so that's good. But her lungs haven't fully developed yet. Hence the steroids. My baby's not even born and she's receiving medical treatment."

"Mrs. Slade, we're ready for you," a nurse in pink scrubs said to Belle.

"I'm just having a routine checkup. I shouldn't be long. Do you want to wait and we can talk?"

Emma nodded. "Yes, thank you."

She sat back in the chair, attempting to remain calm and think logically. How did millions of women give birth every year, just as they had done for thousands of years, without complications? She thought she had done something wrong but the doctor had assured her that snowshoeing and sex weren't to blame.

Neither was her stress. It contributed to her high blood pressure but not the other preterm delivery factors.

As much as Emma wanted to see her little girl, neither one of them was ready. She hated going through this alone. She wanted to call her mom but she couldn't stomach one of her *what's going to be is going to be* speeches. She knew if she called Jennie, her friend would be on the first flight to Montana and insist on staying with her for the next seven weeks. She was that generous of a friend, and Emma wouldn't allow her to jeopardize her job because she was scared.

Belle's exam had taken less time than Emma had anticipated. Harlan was at work and Ivy was visiting her biological mother for the day, allowing Emma and Belle to have the house to themselves.

"How about we make a girl's day out of this?" Belle handed Emma a cup of herbal tea. "We can kick back and watch romantic comedies for the rest of the day."

"I don't think romance is the best thing for me to watch after what happened last night."

"Oh, that." Belle's eyes widened. "Garrett had mentioned that you and Dylan had an argument over the ranch."

"I don't know who I'm madder at. Dylan or myself."

"I don't really understand what happened. Garrett said Dylan had asked him to become his partner on the ranch and you got upset. Full disclosure, he also asked Harlan and Wes to go in with him. Wes said no, but Harlan hasn't made up his mind yet. I think it would be a good idea, but maybe there's something I'm not seeing. Is this about your company not getting the ranch?"

"Yes and no. While I was trying to convince Dylan to sell to me, I decided I wanted to buy into the ranch. Before I had a chance to tell Dylan, he made the offer to his brothers, which I totally understand. While I can't help but be annoyed that he won Garrett over with my ideas, I'm crushed that I gave him three chances to tell me he loved me and he didn't. I told him I thought he would have said the words, and he just stared at me. So, who's the fool? Me? I feel used. He has everything he wants while I get to go home to a demoted position because once this baby is born, I can no longer afford to travel all over the world. That had been my biggest job requirement. So I'm stuck with a paper-pushing job I hate, at least until I find something else. In the meantime, I'm having my baby in Montana and then I have to move into a smaller apartment when I get back to Chicago. This is not the start to my daughter's life that I had expected."

"So he didn't say the words?" Belle asked.

Emma sipped her tea. "The bottom line is, Dylan and I don't trust each other. That came to a head the night Harlan thought I was going behind Dylan's back when I was just doing what my boss had instructed me to do."

"I was furious with him for getting in the middle of that. I am so sorry for the undue stress that put you through."

"I appreciate it, but I understood where Harlan was coming from, too. Dylan had brought me to a particular place on the ranch a few times. A spot Jax had also shown me. The more time I spent there, the more I had envisioned a beautiful open-air wedding chapel where the ranch could provide destination wedding packages."

"Dylan was telling us about them last night. They sound wonderful. I would've loved something like that. Both of my weddings were completely unconventional, and I wouldn't mind a third."

Emma set her teacup on the end table. "Okay, so all those ideas Dylan told you about last night, they were mine. Some had been a part of my original proposal package and the rest, like the chapel, were all ideas I wanted to actively be a part of. The more I thought about them and talked about them, I saw myself helping Dylan see them come to fruition. Not sit on the sidelines and watch him do it with somebody else. Dylan kept asking me to stay in Montana so I naïvely thought he wanted me to be his partner in every way. When I heard him ask Garrett to be his partner instead and then mentioned Harlan and Wes, I was crushed."

Belle patted Emma's thigh. "You got your feelings hurt."

"I sure did. Now that I've had a chance to think about it, maybe I overreacted. In the same respect, I don't know what Dylan expected me to do for work if I said yes and moved to Montana. I'm not the type who would be happy answering phones. Not that there's anything wrong with that, it's just not what I want. I want to be a part of the bigger picture. That has been my job for the last six years. I am a commercial real estate analyst. I make a living looking at the bigger picture. After listening to Dylan, it was obvious he didn't see me the same way. He said he had at one point, but once he took on partners, things were different."

"You wanted to be included." Elvis jumped on the couch between them, spun around a few times and laid down. "The dog gets it. He wants to be included, too."

They both laughed, breaking the tension. Emma scratched the dog behind the ears, only to have him roll over on his back for belly rubs. "I think Dylan believes this is about him not selling the ranch, but it's not. I knew he was going to be a tough sell going in. He has every right to explore his options and ask his family to join him. Although, he already told me Garrett had turned him down once before. If he had said, 'I love you,' I could have overlooked it all. I can't move sixteen hundred miles away from my life for a man who doesn't even know if he loves me."

"I would probably have felt the same way."

Talking to Belle made her feel better. It helped justify her feelings and allowed her to see where she may have been a little too harsh with Dylan. In all actuality, he hadn't really done anything wrong. He was looking out for his best interests. Their relationship had been far too new for either one of them to consider her involvement in the ranch. If anyone had the clearer head, it had probably been Dylan for realizing that fact. That didn't make it any easier to accept.

BELLE WAS THE last person Dylan expected to receive a phone call from that evening. After she had filled him in on Emma's doctor visit, she clarified why Emma was so furious with him. Belle admitted to violating the girl code by telling him all of it, but she felt they both needed to give the other a second chance before giving up completely. Dylan didn't understand how he could have been so blind.

He checked his watch. It wasn't too late to stop by her room. That's if she would open the door for him. He didn't think any amount of singing in the hallway would change her mind this time after the way he had completely disregarded her feelings.

Surprisingly, she answered after the first knock. "Let me guess... Belle."

"She felt horrible for breaking your confidence, but she's worried about you, and so am I. I owe you a huge apology."

"Dylan, it seems like that's all you've done since I've arrived. No more apologies. We have both made mistakes. I invested too much of my heart into this place and I wasn't even aware I was doing it. I don't know if it was you, Jax, Montana or maybe a combination of all of it, but Silver Bells really grabbed ahold of me."

"It tends to have that effect on people."

"I just wish I had seen it before this visit. Maybe I could have prepared myself better."

"The heart wants what the heart wants," Dylan said. "That's the lesson I've learned since you arrived. I thought I had built up enough resistance to protect myself from ever falling in love again. You can't protect yourself from that."

Dylan noticed her suitcases now sat where the Christmas presents had. He scanned the bed and the dresser. There were no blue and pink bags, no baby clothes lying around, no signs of Emma.

"Are you leaving?" Belle had told him Emma was prohibited from traveling.

"I made open-ended reservations in Kalispell. I think it's best if I put some distance between...us."

"I don't want you to go. And I don't think you want to, either."

"Our relationship happened way too fast. Maybe if time had been on our side and we had met under different circumstances, we may have had a chance. I cannot focus on that or worry about it, anymore. My baby may arrive sooner than later. I need to prepare for the fact I'm having my child in Montana. I don't have any of the comforts of home and before you offer, no. I can handle this on my own."

"What about your job?"

"I have made peace with the lesser position. It's relatively stress-free and will allow me to spend more time with my daughter. I have some money to fall back on so we won't have to move right away, but I will have to move soon. It will all work out in the end. I have a job and a roof over my head, I just need to give birth to a healthy baby."

"Emma." Dylan lifted her hands and held them against his chest. "I understand you not wanting to be with me anymore. But I do love you and I still want to be with you."

"Please don't." Emma looked up at him. The life and fire he had once seen in her eyes was gone. "You're only saying that because Belle told you that's what I wanted to hear."

"That's not true. I mean every word. I don't want you to give up on us, but I understand. I wish you would at least stay here, where you don't have to worry about money. It will be one less financial burden. I don't want you to think of it as a gift, I—"

Dylan noticed the cradle and rocking horse on the opposite side of the room away from her luggage. "You are taking those with you, right?"

"Under the circumstances, I don't think I should. They're beautiful and I think you should give them to somebody you plan on spending the rest of your life with. You worked hard on them."

"I built them for your baby. It doesn't matter what happens between us now, tomorrow or ten years from now, these are for your daughter. I want her to have them. You don't have to tell her about me, just…please."

Dylan choked back a tear, an emotion he didn't know he was capable of. He released her hands and stepped away from her. "I will leave you alone now. Just, please, take the cradle and the rocking horse."

Dylan couldn't escape her room fast enough. He ran down the lodge's stairs and into the cold. He couldn't bear the thought of Emma leaving or never seeing her child.

How could he have made so many mistakes?

Chapter Fifteen

Emma hadn't expected saying goodbye would be so difficult the following morning at breakfast. She hated leaving all the wonderful people she'd met and would genuinely miss them. They exchanged numbers and promised to stay in touch. Kalispell wasn't far, so they could still meet on weekends, providing the butter bean cooperated.

Emma wondered if she would see Dylan before she left. It would probably be easier on the two of them if they didn't. She had three and a half hours before her car service arrived. The rental company had already come and picked up her car. In hindsight, she should've done that a week ago.

After breakfast, she headed back to her room. She wished she could have checked into the hotel in Kalispell sooner, but she had to wait until noon.

"Emma." One of the older women who had teased her about Dylan only a few days prior stopped her on the staircase. "Why don't you join us for one last sleigh ride around the ranch before you go? It's just going to be us girls. We've already booked it, and you can be our guest."

"Oh I don't think—"

"Nonsense." The woman hooked her arm in Emma's and steered her back down the stairs. "We have that cowboy hottie, Wes, ready and waiting."

"Oh, okay." Emma allowed the woman to lead her through the lobby. She guessed there wouldn't be any harm since it wasn't Dylan. And how bad could a sleigh ride be with a couple of cowboy-crazy rowdy women? It actually sounded like fun.

The sleigh ride was anything but tame, and Wes egged them on. She had officially heard every dirty joke known to man. Not from Wes. From the women. They even sang dirty songs instead of Christmas carols after stating Christmas was over with and it was time to celebrate being women. Emma began to wonder just how much celebrating they had done before embarking on their little adventure.

Even though her group of rebels was far from romantic, Emma couldn't help but think about the many sleigh rides she had taken with Dylan. She missed him already and she hadn't even stepped foot off the ranch. When Wes reined the sleigh to a stop at the location she and Dylan had made love, Emma thought her heart would shatter into a million pieces.

In the distance, a single draft horse and sleigh approached. To her surprise, it was Dylan. He stepped out of the sleigh and walked toward her, carrying a bouquet of long-stemmed red roses. Wordlessly, he took her gloved hand, helped her out of the sleigh and led her to the future chapel site. The sound of sleigh bells jingled behind them, as Wes and company drove away.

"You all had this planned, didn't you?" Emma asked.

"Yes, ma'am." Dylan tipped his hat. "I couldn't let you leave without showing you how much you and your baby mean to me. I've spent most of my thirty-five years alone. Even though I wanted a family to call my own, I never saw it in my future. And I know your little butter bean isn't mine biologically, but I have this unexplainable attachment to her mother and that automatically led me to fall in love with her, too."

"Dylan, what are you saying?" Emma clutched the roses to her chest.

"I'm saying I love you, Emma Sheridan. I don't want to spend another day without you by my side. I have been so stubborn and pigheaded that I haven't truly seen what is right in front of me. I don't want you to go to Kalispell today. I don't want you to go back to Chicago once your daughter is born. I want you to stay. Here. In Montana with me." Dylan reached into his pocket and knelt in the snow on one knee. "As my wife." He held a diamond ring in front of him. "Will you marry me?"

"Dylan, I'm having a baby," Emma said as tears stung her cheeks.

"And I want to be a part of her life. I want to raise her as my own."

"No." Emma gripped his shoulder. "I'm having a baby. Now!"

"Holy crap!" Dylan pocketed the ring and sprang to his feet. He swept her into his arms and carried her to the sleigh, bundling her in blankets before taking the reins. "It's going to be all right. I'll take care of you. I promise nothing will happen to you or the butter bean."

BY THE TIME they reached the hospital, Dylan thought he would have a heart attack.

"I should have taken Lamaze classes." Emma said as they wheeled her down the hallway. "I should've learned how to breathe properly." Dylan ran beside her as she squeezed the life out of his hand. "I'm sorry I ruined your proposal."

"Don't worry about that. There can always be another proposal. There's only one butter bean."

"Oh, God!" She screamed as she doubled over in pain. "My baby is coming and I still don't have a name." They reached the delivery room and two women in pink scrubs helped her out of the wheelchair and into a gown.

"Is the father staying for the delivery?" one of the women asked Emma.

"Oh, I'm not the father." As much as he would love to be in the room for the delivery, he didn't want Emma to feel uncomfortable.

"Yes, he is." Emma winced as they eased her onto the bed. "You are her father. I accept your proposal."

"You do?" Dylan ran to her side, unfamiliar tears wetting his cheeks. "You just made me the happiest man alive."

"Okay, Mr. Happy. We need to get you in a gown, booties and a cap." Dylan felt himself being spun in multiple directions. He'd never been in a delivery room before, let alone a delivery room where he was about to become a father.

"Oh, my God, I'm going to be a dad."

Emma smiled weakly at him from across the room. "Would you please finish getting dressed and get back over here." It was more of a demand than a question. And he was more than willing to oblige. Dylan bent down and kissed Emma softly on the forehead. "You're doing good, honey. You're about to be a mom."

"Are you sure you want this? Are you sure you want this responsibility for the next eighteen years?"

The idea alone should have terrified him, but he welcomed it. He wanted a family with Emma more than anything else in this world. "There's no one else I would rather spend my life with."

"Okay, Emma," the doctor said. "This baby is coming quickly. I'm going to need you to give me a couple of good pushes when I say so. Are you ready?"

"No." Emma shook her head. "I don't even have a name for her."

The doctor laughed. "You're not the first person that's happened to. You'll figure it out. Now I need you to give me a push on the count of three. One. Two. Push."

Emma squeezed Dylan's hand even tighter as she tried to sit up and push at the same time.

"Keep an eye on her blood pressure," the doctor

said to one of the nurses. "Emma, I'm going to need you to push again. She's almost here. On the count of three. One. Two. Push."

Emma pushed again, her breaths more ragged as one of the machines began beeping wildly. Dylan read the concern in the doctor's eyes.

"You can do this, baby, you can do this, baby," he reassured.

"I'm so tired." Emma looked up at him. "I don't think I can." Fear was etched across her delicate features.

"You *can* do this. I have faith in you. I'm right here by your side. You look at me. You look into my eyes and you don't stop looking into my eyes until that baby is born."

"Okay, Emma, this is the last one. I need you to push or we're going to have to deliver this baby by cesarean. On the count of three. One. Two."

"Push," Dylan said in unison with the doctor. "Push, Emma. Push."

"There we go," the doctor said. The sound of a baby's cry reverberated throughout the room as the doctor held her up for Emma to see. "Dad, would you like to cut the cord?"

Dylan nodded, unable to speak. A nurse handed him the scissors, instructing him to cut between the clamps. She was so tiny, but not as tiny as he had feared. And she had a mop of brown hair, just like her mom's.

"She's beautiful, Emma."

"I want to hold her." She reached out her arms.

The doctor carried the infant to a small, padded table and laid her under a heat lamp as a nurse began rubbing her vigorously with a towel. "We're going to clean and examine your daughter. We need to make sure she's healthy since she's six-and-a-half weeks premature."

"Is she okay?" Emma struggled to sit up. "Tell me! Is my baby okay?" Panic crept into her voice.

"Shh, sweetheart. They're taking good care of her." The wait seemed endless as a small team gathered around the table. Dylan had never known fear until this moment. And he hadn't known he was capable of a love so deep.

The doctor returned, carrying a pink swaddled bundle. "Mama, meet your daughter." She placed her in Emma's arms. "We'll need to run more tests in a few minutes, but she's doing great."

Tears spilled down Emma's cheeks as she held her baby. "Hello, Holly. I'm your mommy."

"I CAN'T BELIEVE you're actually here." Emma cradled her daughter. "My beautiful girl." After numerous tests, they had assured her Holly was healthy. Emma couldn't believe how blessed she was.

"She's beautiful, just like you." Dylan brushed Emma's hair away from her face. "And I love her name."

"Holly Jax Slade. I don't remember ever seeing Holly in a baby book, so I'm not sure where I got the idea for the name but somehow it fits. I think it was all that Christmas spirit you showed me. And Jax," she sighed. "He had to be a part of this somehow. I swear he was watching over her today."

"I still can't believe she has my last name." Dylan beamed proudly beside them.

"And I can't believe I'm going to be your wife. Speaking of which, whatever happened to that ring you were going to slide on my finger?"

Dylan reached into his pocket and pulled it out. "It's right here, future Mrs. Slade." Dylan held her hand in his. "Now are you sure about this?"

"Oh, I'm definitely sure I want to be your wife and raise our daughter together," Emma said as he slid the ring on her finger.

* * * * *

If you enjoyed this book,
don't miss the next book in Amanda Renee's
SADDLE RIDGE, MONTANA *series,*
WRANGLING CUPID'S COWBOY,
available January 2018
from Mills & Boon!

MILLS & BOON®

Cherish™

EXPERIENCE THE ULTIMATE RUSH OF FALLING IN LOVE

A sneak peek at next month's titles...

In stores from 16th November 2017:

- **Married Till Christmas** – Christine Rimmer *and*
  Christmas Bride for the Boss – Kate Hardy
- **The Maverick's Midnight Proposal** – Brenda Harlen
  and **The Magnate's Holiday Proposal** –
  Rebecca Winters

In stores from 30th November 2017:

- **Yuletide Baby Bargain** – Allison Leigh *and*
  The Billionaire's Christmas Baby – Marion Lennox
- **Christmastime Courtship** – Marie Ferrarella *and*
  Snowed in with the Reluctant Tycoon – Nina Singh

Just can't wait?
Buy our books online before they hit the shops!
www.millsandboon.co.uk

Also available as eBooks.

MILLS & BOON®

EXCLUSIVE EXTRACT

With just days until Christmas, gorgeous but bewildered billionaire Max Grayland needs hotel maid Sunny Raye's help caring for his baby sister Phoebe. She agrees – only if they spend Christmas with her family!

Read on for a sneak preview of
THE BILLIONAIRE'S CHRISTMAS BABY

'Miss Raye, would you be prepared to stay on over Christmas?'

Oh, for heaven's sake…

To miss Christmas… Who were they kidding?

'No,' she said blankly. 'My family's waiting.'

'But Mr Grayland's stranded in an unknown country, staying in a hotel for Christmas with a baby he didn't know existed until yesterday.' The manager's voice was urbane, persuasive, doing what he did best. 'You must see how hard that will be for him.'

'I imagine it will be,' she muttered and clung to her chocolates. And to her Christmas. 'But it's…'

Max broke in. 'But if there's anything that could persuade you… I'll double what the hotel will pay you. Multiply it by ten if you like.'

Multiply by ten… If it wasn't Christmas…

But it was Christmas. Gran and Pa were waiting. She had no choice.

But other factors were starting to niggle now. Behind Max, she could see tiny Phoebe lying in her too-big cot. She'd pushed herself out of her swaddle and was waving her tiny hands in desperation. Her face was red with screaming.

She was so tiny. She needed to be hugged, cradled, told all was right with her world. Despite herself, Sunny's heart twisted.

But to forgo Christmas? *No way.*

'I can't,' she told him, still hugging her chocolates. But then she met Max's gaze. This man was in charge of his world but he looked…desperate. The pressure in her head was suddenly overwhelming.

And she made a decision. What she was about to say was ridiculous, crazy, but the sight of those tiny waving arms, that red, desperate face was doing something to her she didn't understand and the words were out practically before she knew she'd utter them.

'Here's my only suggestion,' she told them. 'If you really do want my help… My Gran and Pa live in a big old house in the outer suburbs. It's nothing fancy; in fact it's pretty much falling down. It might be dilapidated but it's huge. So no, Mr Grayland, I won't spend Christmas here with you, but if you're desperate, if you truly think you can't manage Phoebe alone, then you're welcome to join us until you can make other arrangements. You can stay here and take care of Phoebe yourself, you can make other arrangements or you can come home with me. Take it or leave it.'

Don't miss
THE BILLIONAIRE'S CHRISTMAS BABY
by Marion Lennox

Available December 2017
www.millsandboon.co.uk

Join Britain's BIGGEST Romance Book Club

- **EXCLUSIVE offers every month**
- **FREE delivery direct to your door**
- **NEVER MISS a title**

Call Customer Services
0844 844 1358*

or visit
millsandboon.co.uk/bookclub

* This call will cost you 7 pence per minute plus your
phone company's price per minute access charge.

BKCB4